All Hallows Angel

Chelle Renee

ISBN: 153323700X
ISBN 13: 9781533237002

All Hallows Angel

Emily finds her daddy an unlikely angel in a shy girl from Louisiana who was suspected to be harboring a fugitive in New York.

Prologue

"Daddy, daddy, daddy, I'm sooooo sorry, I didn't mean it, I can't believe it's gone, I'm sooooo sorry!"

"Emily, what the---" Jack got hold of his words before blurting out something he really didn't want his six year old to repeat. Groggily he rubbed his tired eyes and ran a hand through his disheveled hair while sitting up and pulling his weeping daughter into his lap.

"Now Angel, what is it that has you running and screaming into my room at this time of the morning?"

Jack then realized that it was not light out yet and one glance at his alarm clock told him it was barely four in the morning. His daughter was shuddering and crying in his arms with her blond head tucked into his chest.

More than a little anxious about his daughter's sudden outburst, a flood of 'what ifs' ran through his head. He hadn't remembered the phone ringing, and from his quick assessment before she tucked herself into a tight ball against him, he determined that she was in no physical harm that he could tell. Jack was always anxious about his daughter asking about her mother, especially now that she was in school. When all the other mothers picked up their bubbly brood at the bus stop he always felt more than a little out of place, and always harbored the fear that Emily would start asking questions about her absentee Mother.... Questions Jack was reluctant to answer....Questions Jack had no answers for.

Last night had been fun for both him and Emily. Dressed as the prettiest Angel Jack had ever laid eyes upon, Emily drug him from house to house in their small Louisiana town of Lacassine, until returning to their safe haven at the end of the cul-de-sac. Emily loved Halloween and had talked Jack into driving all over their small town in search for the coveted array of sugary treats that would keep her hopping for weeks to come. Their last stops had been in their neighborhood, making sure to stop at each and every house in the cul-de-sac before daring to come home. Barely in the door with her proud earnings in tow, Emily soon fell fast asleep on the couch while examining her feast.

Jack had carried his sleeping angel, shiny halo and all, and laid her in her bed just after ten last night, and he knew that she would be out until at least seven in the morning on any normal Saturday. Saturday was Jack and Emily's special day to lounge in front of the television for hours eating cereal right out of the box and not getting out of their pajamas until noon. After that they would decide what they would do for their special daddy –daughter day. Being Jacks only day off from work he looked forward to sleeping in (if you could call seven in the morning 'sleeping in'), and spending the day with his special little girl.

"Baby, what is the matter, daddy will fix it, it can't possibly be that terrible. Let me see your pretty face." Jack tried to console his daughter all the while chastising his own fears in the back of his mind.

Slowly Emily raised her sobbing face to look up at Jack. She was still wearing her white angel costume and still had glitter in her blond hair and on her face. Jack said a silent prayer thanking God that he didn't have to work that day. The boys at the Lodge sure would get a kick out of the 'pretty sparkles' he was sure were now all over his neck and face too.

Emily had made sure she was the angel who had the most 'pretty sparkles' that anyone had ever seen.

"Daddy, you know that angels need to have pretty things right?" She asked.

Jack nodded his confused head.

"Well, Daddy, I found a ring to wear that was so pretty. I knew it had to belong to an angel, and I was only borrowing it for my costume, but I lost it Daddy, it's gone." At that Emily started crying again and sniffled repeatedly as she tried to catch her breath.

"Honey, Daddy is confused, where did you find this ring, at school? At Grandmas? Aunt Monicas? Because honey you know it's not nice to take things that aren't yours." He said, straining to lean closer, to kiss the top of her head.

"I know daddy, but I was just borrowing it." Peeking up at him again with one eye open she said, "Then I was going to put it back in your sock drawer where I found it."

1

(Six Years Earlier)

"**D**ude, when are you going to grow up and realize that she is not coming back? It's been over two weeks! That little girl needs something more than four frat boys. The Dean is going to kick you out when he realizes she is here. And he will realize it! You know inspection week is coming up. You need to take her to your mothers, or her mothers. You can't seriously be thinking of keeping her around!"

"Shut up, just shut up! I have been hearing this over and over again. She is my daughter and her mother said she would be back. I know her, she will keep her word. We are in love. I am going to marry that girl!" Jack said as he picked up the little bundle he was scared to death of. There was no way he was going to tell these guys that, but their words were what kept him up at night. He knew he was in way over his head.

Three sets of eyes rolled at that statement. Jeff, Jim, and Clayton had been trying endlessly to talk sense into their boy ever since Mystique Left that little girl on their doorstep and hightailed it out of there.

"That girl saw an opportunity to get out of her responsibilities, dumped them on you, and dropped you like a hot poker!" Clayton said.

"That's not the way it went down and you know it!" Jack exclaimed.

"Might as well have been," Clayton replied, "She didn't even tell you about her for the week she was hiding out here. How the hell do you explain that one?"

Jeff and Jim were tired of the back and forth that seemed endless with these two lately. A twelve pack and PlayStation kept them entertained as they tried to ignore the shouts from their buddies and drown out the whimpering that was starting again from Emily. Neither was thrilled about her being there, but Jacks Dad being the Assistant Wrestling Coach had got them in good standing with the school board. Neither was going to chance pissing him off and risk losing their scholarships.

Emily's Mother, Mystique, and Jack had met during her freshman orientation the fall of his junior year. Jack had been assigned to take some of the potential freshmen that would be starting in the following spring and introduce them to some of the extracurriculars the school offered. Jack had twenty potential students assigned to him yet he had only had eyes for one shy petite blond that tried her best to blend into the background and not be noticed. Try as she might, she could not avoid the attention from Jack. With her slender legs, not quite hidden by the long flowing baby blue whisper of a sheer skirt, and skin that glowed like ripe peaches, Jack found himself mesmerized by her. Soon after showing them around the campus and introducing them to some of the more laid back aspects of campus life Jack found himself hypnotized with Mystique. Her eyes had lit up when he showed them around the jazz clubs, karaoke bars, 24hr fitness center with Olympic sized pool, creative arts center, and coffee houses. Of course Jack had also introduced them all to the ball coaches, and club leaders, but he was a student and knew that students were often more interested in life outside of what had to be done for the school. He thought he could literally see her exhale as the tour of the "fun" side of campus life meandered on.

Jack had made it a point to stand in her way as she wandered toward the exit. Noticing that she was trying her best not to make eye contact Jack plastered on his biggest beaming smile and extended his hand just before she made it to the front door of the coffee shop he had taken them to as a last stop on the tour.

"Hi, I'm Jack." He said.

Smiling sweetly she said, "I know, you introduced yourself at the beginning of the tour."

"Oh, um, I, uh, forgot," Jack stammered.

"That's ok." She said as she quickly walked past him trying to make her retreat.

"Uh wait," Jack called as he jogged toward her, "Are you doing anything right now?"

"I was going home to help my Parents." Mystique stated bluntly.

"Help them do what?" He asked.

"I'm sorry; did you need me for something else? I thought the tour was over, most everyone else has left." she said, while glancing around the parking lot, and avoiding his question.

"Don't worry, I'm not some crazed lunatic, and the tour is over," Jack smiled at her again giving her his best 'I'm interested in you, but please don't think of me as an attacker', crooked grin. "I was just thinking of what I was going to do for supper, and I thought it might be nice to have some company from a potential incoming freshman." After hesitating a few seconds longer her added, "But, I see that you are backing away from me and looking for an escape, so I guess I blew my chances."

Mystique glanced at her watch and then back to him. "I guess that would be ok, but you really don't have to do that, after tonight's tour I will probably still go to school here, you don't have to keep being nice just to draw in students."

Jack smiled at her and offered his elbow as a friendly gesture.

"Just doing my job ma'am, just doing my Job!" he said.

Of course they both laughed at that first awkward meeting every time someone had asked them how they got together. Jacks friends never let him live down how he coerced an innocent girl by getting her to go to LSU by showing her the "extracurriculars."

Jack and Mystique had a whirlwind of a relationship. If was passionate and crazy and over before he knew what had happened. After that first meeting they began to see each other on a regular basis and their relationship really heated up when she began attending school there the next semester.

Mystique was thrilled to be out from her parent's shadow. They were definitely hippies in all aspects of their lives, from solar power, home grown everything, handmade clothes (when they wore them), astrological readings, a vegan diet, and those were just the 'normal' hippie things they did, according to her. She was embarrassed to tell him, on that first night, she was in a hurry to get home because she had to walk since her parents didn't believe in polluting the earth with the use of motorized vehicles, and that she was going to help them set up for a coven meeting.

Having been homeschooled she had to hurry and get her GED so that she could take the SAT's and get enrolled in spring semester. Her parents only allowed this after much pleading and begging on her part. The tour of the extracurricular activities really sealed the deal with them. They were still extremely skeptical of any formal education but decided to let her go when she showed them brochures that showed there was yoga, dance, poetry readings, even an astrology club.

That spring Mystique moved into the girls dormitory which was across campus from Jack, but he was glad to have her on the grounds and the few blocks that separated their living quarters didn't keep them apart in the least. Whenever there was a spare moment they would find themselves in each other's arms. More often than not Jacks roommates would find themselves in a precarious situation when they stumbled around half dressed in the mornings only to find Mystique still sleeping on Jacks bunk or sneaking out of the frat house after having stayed the night with Jack.

Although it had been unique, Mystique had led a very sheltered life up until that spring. She loved her new-found freedom at school, and her and Jacks lives were endlessly intertwined in seemed. Jacks parents adored the petite flower that Jack was infatuated with, and even Mystiques parents were opening up to the idea of their little girl growing into a mature woman and discovering the world beyond where she had always been.

Jack and Mystique had a long spring break that semester and decided to spend some quality alone time together. Although it was quite new the four and a half month relationship felt right to both of them. They had talked about running off to Vegas and eloping, or maybe just finding a small wedding chapel somewhere and securing what they both felt was right in their young hearts.

So what went wrong? Jack thought to himself as he watched his little girl finally drifting off to dreamland. Throwing himself back against his bed he stared up at the stucco ceiling hoping to find some revelation or answers to the thoughts that had been plaguing him.

Jack and Mystique never made the spring break trip they had been planning. The morning before they were to leave Jack took his excited fiancée to the best Jeweler he could afford on his meager part time wages from the Gap. They browsed hand in hand for over an hour before deciding on a beautiful princess cut diamond surrounded by platinum rose petals. Jack knew he would have to work major overtime to pay for it, but the look on Mystiques face told him it was worth it.

Jack picked up the ring from the Jeweler the next morning, after having the final cleaning and appraisal. Then he was off to Mystiques dorm to greet her with it and a dozen red roses. He was on cloud nine. No one knew they were planning to elope. They had planned to share the news with their families and friends when they returned.

Jacks face fell and he felt like he had swallowed a brick when he opened the dorm room door and found himself staring at the grim faces of her roommates. No one said a word as he walked through the door and noticed her dresser was cleared out and her bedding was gone. One of her roommates started sobbing and the other just turned and walked away. Jack thought the worst at first until he saw her handwriting on the little marker board they kept by the desk.

'Sorry, I just can't take this anymore, I'm going back home.'--Mystique

Jack threw the roses on her bare bed and left without saying a word to either girl.

He spent the next few months in a daze. He did manage to keep up his school work and put in a lot of extra time at his part time job. He even finished first in his weight class at all the remaining wrestling events that spring. He found that sleep was barely an option after the crushing blow that left a gaping hole in his heart, so he kept himself busy and finished out his junior year with honors. His parents were proud, but Jacks buddies knew there was something not right about his behavior.

Jack and his three frat buddies spent the summer road tripping across the US. They were all going into their senior year and knew that real life was going to catch up with them sooner than later.

By the time they moved back into the frat house the next fall Jack had managed to pull himself out of his funk for the most part. He had not seen Mystique in the city anywhere over the summer and had not heard from her since the day they picked out the ring he still kept hidden away in his dresser.

Jack, Jim, Jeff, and Clayton made up the wrestling team that fall, and Jacks Dad was proud of them giving LSU such a sendoff their senior year, and his last year coaching before retirement.

Jack gave up on the idea of Mystique coming back into his life and decided that things were going pretty good for him. He was sleeping again and even went on a date or two. Nothing serious, but at least he was moving on with his life. By the last semester of his senior year he was feeling like new again.

— —

Everything changed for him the last week in January and now he had some important decisions to make. Jack sat up and tried to rub his temples to try and make it all make sense. Reaching into his back pocket he pulled out his phone, took a picture of his sleeping daughter and sent it along with a text to his older sister Monica saying, 'we need to talk.'

Jack explained to Monica how Mystique had come back into his life just a few weeks ago. She had told him that school and the thought of getting married had scared her and she ran. She told him again and again how sorry she was that she had not contacted him or talked to him about her fears. She begged him for forgiveness and he thought they were going to be a couple again. Then she dropped the bombshell of his daughter on him and she was gone the next day, but Emily was there to stay. He was devastated that things with him and Mystique had gone so wrong, but Emily was a treasure that he didn't even know he wanted until she was his. 'Finer than the rarest diamonds and more beautiful than the purest gold,' was the phrase he used to describe her to Monica. She laughed at the description he chose for his daughter, but was pleased to know that her brother was growing up. Monica made sure to ask about a paternity test as tactfully as she could, and found herself relieved and even excited about her niece.

Two hours and a lot of tears later Jack was packing up his little girl to take her to meet her Aunt and Grandparents for the first time. He decided with only a few months left in the semester before graduation he needed to focus on his studies, and let his roommates off the hook from being caught with an infant to explain to the school board. If they didn't need a forth roommate to keep their fraternity name Jack would have moved back home to finish up his schooling. It was hard but Jack knew that Monica and his parents would make a good home for her until he graduated and found a place to live.

"Thanks Man, I will be back in a few days." Jack said as Clayton handed him the last of Emily's things to be put in the back of his blazer.

"Don't worry, this isn't forever, you are not running out on her, you will graduate soon and you already have that job lined up at the Lodge. You are going to give her a future, and you are a great Dad." Clayton said.

"Alright, enough with the mushy stuff, you better have a beer waiting for me when I get back!" Jack said after sighing through his frustration.

"I will, a case of it, and by the way tell your hot sister 'hi' for me!" Clayton said with a grin as he jumped away from the mock punch Jack threw his way.

Jack didn't comment as he got in the driver's seat to make his way to his parents' house. Big blue eyes looked innocently at him from the back seat as he leaned back to check on Emily once more before embarking on their destination.

"Daddy loves you Angel." He whispered before turning back around to face what had to be done.

2

(Present day)

"Put on your fairy wings honey!" Angela's mother chimed as she flitted by for the umpteenth time to make sure everything was just how she wanted it; candy in place, decorations scary but cute at the same time.

"Mom, I have only been home for an hour, I am not in the mood for your Halloween bizarre!" She huffed at her mother.

"Sweetie, I am not going to argue with you, just put on your wings and your smile and you will feel better before you know it." Her mother said with a big glossy smile as she tucked the hair behind Angela's ears and wiped a smudge off her face.

"Leave her alone Gretchen and quit your fretting!" Angela's father, Ken, exclaimed as he grabbed her mother's hand and pulled her down on his rather ample lap.

Gretchen had always been a nervous person, thin as a rail and always on the go. Angela barely remembers her Mother sitting at a family meal or gathering. She seemed to always be on her feet primping and prodding to make sure everything was just right so that everyone had everything they needed to make the event go smoothly.

Angela's Father was more of a laid back teddy bear, not only in size but his nature as well.

"Relax and give your Frankenstein some sugar my little bride, and later after the trick-or-treaters are gone....." he said aloud before drifting off into an array of whispers that only her mother could hear, all of which made her giggle and blush and turn into a puddle of goo in her husband's arms.

Angela groaned for the second time since arriving as she heard her father and mother drift off into their own little world of whispered promises and stolen kisses.

Her parents had always been a very affectionate couple. Angela was already doubting her decision to move back home, even if it was only until she was back on her feet and had her ex out of her life and out of her overwhelmed mind.

Gretchen giggled once more before pinching her husband on the chin while hopping up exclaiming, "Ken there will be plenty of time for that later after the trick or treaters leave. Right now you have to make sure you haunted house is ready and I have to get these treat bags and punch ready!"

Ken rolled his eyes and looked at his daughter. "Let's get going sweetie before you mom has an aneurysm!"

Angela sighed and stood up to follow her dad who was already hauling the majority of her bags up the stairs toward her bedroom.

Angela was leery of moving back home. In her mind it felt like defeat. She had gone to school in New York to be a fashion designer. She had loved getting out of her small Louisiana town and getting a taste of the rest of the world. That was until it bit her in the ass. Angela had only one more year left in design school and already had offers from Gucci to come work for them as a designer once she graduated.

She was ecstatic that Gucci would want her as a designer. Coming from a small town she was sure she would have to work even harder to get her designs noticed. It seemed like a miracle when she was approached by a fashion scout after leaving class one day. Evan Dubair had come from

Paris to work for Gucci and told Angela he had been auditing her class for his company and thought she had a good eye for how things should look, liked her use of color, and saw great potential in her designs. She soon became infatuated with the sleek fashion scout who had literally charmed the pants off of her. Before she knew what had happened he had moved into her small downtown apartment with her, (claiming he wanted to get a taste of 'the real New York') Evan even took her to Paris for a long weekend sabbatical so that she could get a feel for the culture in the fashion capital of the world.

Angela was quite smitten with Evan and more than a little flattered that such a worldly man would be interested in a simple small town girl like herself. Despite the nagging underlying gut feeling of doubt that she had when she first met him, Angela put Evan on a pedestal right next to the one he had her on.

At least Angela thought she was riding high on that pedestal. Evan told her he was talking her up to Gucci and made promises of introducing her as soon as the next semester started, because according to him they couldn't "officially" talk to her about coming to work for them until she was at least started with the last semester, and showed promise of graduating in the near future. Angela had fallen head over heels for the debonair Frenchman who made her swoon with every coy look he threw her way. Evan took her to fancy restaurants and dazzled her with his sophisticated charms. She was so trusting of him that she had cancelled plans to come home that Winter and was planning on staying in New York so that they could spend some time together without college and Evans job getting in the way, as he planned to take his vacation time over her winter break from classes.

Angela had chalked up the initial gut feelings of doom to her already overwhelming feelings of big city jitters. She had been in New York for over three years and had made some good friends, but anything new still made her a little uneasy.

It was just little things, she would tell herself, whenever her friends would mention that they didn't trust Evan or that they had a bad feeling about him. But, he always had a good reason for his behaviors. He said he was stand-offish because he was shy and from a different country and culture. He moved in with her in her little one-bedroom apartment and gave up his car so that he could get a feel for city life and how New Yorkers lived and went about their day to day lives. Even when they went to Paris he had talked her into using her frequent flyer miles, but he paid for the rest of the trip so she thought nothing of it.

Angela was happy in her relationship with him and believed that Evan only had good intentions with her. She was ecstatic to be involved with such a suave man, and was looking forward to starting a career with Gucci.

Everything in her life seemed to be falling into place until one night in mid-October when she had decided to order a pizza for her and her good friend to have a rare "girls night " in. Evan was out of town on business and the girls took full advantage of lounging in their sweats and forgoing the makeup. They had rented tear-jerking chick flicks, had two bottles of chardonnay chilled, and more cookie dough than they could consume in the course of the evening.

When the doorbell rang Angela grabbed her purse and that's when she realized she had forgotten to stop at the ATM that morning as planned. Betty didn't have any cash on her either. The girls ran around her cramped little apartment frantically looking for any cash that might be stashed away that she had forgotten about. When Betty came out of the bedroom with Evans wallet the girls knew they were saved and their cheesy treat wouldn't be taken away.

Angela wasn't in the least worried that he had forgotten his wallet, because he was in fashion and he had told her once that he liked to switch out his wallets to match his suits. At least that was his explanation when she questioned him about having so many in his briefcase. However she wasn't expecting the surprise waiting for her when she casually flung it open and went to grab some cash from inside. It was certainly Evans face that stared back at her, but the name was all wrong. The confusion stopped Angela in her tracks and her friend rushed to her side just as she sat hard on the shag carpeting that covered her little living room floor.

"He's waiting for his money Ang...." was all she could get out before seeing the vacant stare in her friends eyes as she turned white as a ghost.

'What, oh, here, take it." She mumbled as she handed Betty the wallet that suddenly felt like hot coals in her ice cold hand.

Betty looked at Angela strangely as she took out a twenty and told the delivery boy to keep the change. For the most part Evan had taken her friend from her except on these special occasions when he was nowhere to be found. He certainly could afford to give a three dollar tip to the delivery boy who seemed especially grateful to get it.

When he was gone she sat the pizza on the end table and rushed back to Angela's side.

"What is the matter with you?" She asked exasperated.

"He's not Evan." was all she kept repeating over and over, not focusing on anything in particular, but rocking back and forth while hugging her knees close to her chest.

It took Betty a few minutes to realize how this all started and she slowly opened up the wallet. Her heart sank for her friend as she saw Dewar Grant from Pensacola FL looking back at her.

When Angela finally got up the nerve to call Evan he tried to make light of the situation. Dewar was his actual name, he told her, but he did better in the fashion world when he went by Evan Dubair. He was quite the smooth talker and almost had her convinced until she asked him where he was really from and he told her Miami. When asked why his ID said he was from Pensacola he became flustered and would not answer any more of her questions. Angela then told him she didn't want him to come back except to pick up his belongings which he could do at the front desk downstairs.

Angela was shocked at his sudden turn around when he said, "I made you who you are Bitch! You will never be anyone in this town after I get done telling Gucci what a backwoods rag muffin you really are!" At that he ended the call.

With tears blurring her vision both physically and mentally Angela packed up her own meager belongings and caught the next bus back to her hometown in Louisiana. She didn't quite understand who or what he was but she had been so shaken by Evans abrupt outburst and the fact that her world was suddenly turned upside down that she knew she couldn't stay in New York any longer. She just couldn't fit into the crazy world she was suddenly thrust into.

As Angela stared at her reflection in the childhood mirror up top of the white wicker dresser that covered one wall of her quaint little bedroom, she was horrified to see the woman that was looking back at her. Angela did not recognize this drab woman with her sunken cheeks and dark circles under her almond eyes, nor did she notice when her mother came in the room and quietly sat down in the chair across from her bed. Looking into the eyes that stared back at her she wondered just what happened to that naïve young lady that left this very room not much more than three years earlier. What happened to the girl who was head of the cheer squad or leader in the church children's choir all through high school? There were mostly only girls in the choir and they would love having sleepovers at Angela's house. They would play dress up and do each other's hair and nails. Angela had always wanted to be a fashion designer, or so she thought. She loved dressing the little girls up in her clothes and she loved how happy it made her and her friends feel after they spent the day getting pampered and made over. Now she was re-thinking her whole career choice. *Maybe it was just the time spent with those little girls and good friends and not the new clothes that made us feel so good about ourselves.* She thought to herself. As the tears started to flow down her cheeks her mother stood up and went to her side. Shocked, Angela drew in her breath and looked up at the concerned woman who had always been there for her.

"Mom, I am so sorry." Was all she could manage to utter between sobs.

"Baby, it's ok, you will bounce back and be stronger for it. I know my little girl and she can do anything she sets her mind to!" Gretchen consoled.

"Mom, I'm not such a little girl anymore, and that's not true, I didn't make it in New York, I left with my tail between my legs." She said.

"That's not the way I see it honey. You tried it out and came to your senses when you realized that was not the life for you. It took courage to come back home and start over. Don't let me hear you putting my little girl down!" Her mother spoke with certainty.

"Oh mom, I know you are probably right, but I feel like such a failure. I didn't even finish my degree, what am I going to do now?" She wept as she hugged her mother tight.

Wiping the tears from her cheek Gretchen said to her daughter, "you will do anything you set your mind to because you are my daughter and you are a strong independent woman."

Angela gave her mother a half smile. It was nice to know that her mother had so much faith in her, even more so than she had in herself. She was grateful for both her parents not making her feel bad about moving back in with them after she had barely spoken to them in the months that her and Evan had been together. They never even once gave her an 'I told you so,' and didn't even ask specific details about why she needed to move back home. Angela had simply told her Mother and Father the bare facts of what happened and they welcomed her back with open arms.

"Ok mom, let's get your party started, where are my fairy wings?" She said as she stood to face whatever life had in store for her from that moment on.

Angela found herself enjoying the trick-or-treaters more than she expected to. She had perched her fairy clad self in a comfortable chair next to the front door with a big black cauldron full of treats to divvy out to all the children decked out in their Halloween duds.

3

"Emily and I have looked all over for it! It's nowhere to be found!" Jack told his sister Monica as he handed her back the metal detector. She found it almost funny to see him walking up and down the streets of their small town like a foolhardy prospector with the metal detector in hand. He had given it to her for her birthday one year when she had taken a trip to Arkansas to go mining. She didn't have the heart to tell him that she didn't want the thing and had only gone on the trip to be with her boyfriend at the time. She was glad to see someone finally getting some use out of it, but was disheartened that he was looking so hard to find the lost engagement ring from Emily's long-lost mother. She hadn't wanted it, why did Jack?

"She sees you, you know." Monica replied.

With a blank stare on his face he looked up at her and growled, "What the hell are you talking about!"

"Emily is beside herself. She is so sad that she's let you down she doesn't even want to play with her dolls anymore!" Monica snapped back.

"Well she should be upset. She went into my personal space and took something without permission." He said

"Now little brother you know that isn't the whole truth! You let that little girl play dress up all the time. She is always in your things and you have never reacted like this before. What is it? Tell me the truth!"

"I don't know what you think you are getting at Mon, she needs to learn to leave things be and that there are consequences for her actions!" Jack huffed as he stood up and started pacing around the table in his sisters cramped kitchen. Whenever Jack was in need of comfort he ran to Monica's for advice. He knew she could see through his bullshit and get him to admit to her and himself what was really going on in that thick head of his.

"What I'm getting at, Jack," she said as she stood up and put her hands on his shoulders to get his attention, "is that you aren't really mad at Emily, you are mad at the situation, and you have been for years. You need to let it go. No matter how tough it is, you have to move on for her sake and for yours!"

"How do I do that Monica?" He said shaking his head and plopping back down in the hard chrome backed chair.

"Well, first you have to accept the fact that Mystique is not coming back. It has been six years. It is ok to move on." She tried to say with as much empathy as she could muster.

"I know, dammit, I know." He said as he slapped both his hands hard on the table.

"The truth is, that is all I can give her that was her Mothers, and now it is gone. I'm not mad at her, I'm mad at me, you are right about that. I should have given her the ring years ago, but I am afraid of the questions she will have. How do I tell that sweet little girl that her Mother up and left her?"

Monica took a few minutes before answering him and said, "That is just too bad for her. She missed out on the chance to know a beautiful and precious child. But, Jack she is a happy child and knows that she is loved. You can't take away what you can be for her, because of what you can't be for her. Right now she is feeling scared and confused and needs to know that her Daddy loves her and forgives her. You're right that she needs more boundaries and needs to know that she can't be going through things that don't belong to her, but she was only doing what she has been taught. Right now you need to teach her that she has one great parent that she can count on no matter what! And," she paused for a few seconds before saying, "while you're at it you might want to watch your mouth, you never know when her little ears might hear you."

Jack just stared at her for a minute letting it all sink in before saying, "Thanks sis, you always know how to explain things when I get to thinking too much."

"Ok, enough of that lets get these pies out of the oven so that they will be cool when Emily gets off the bus." Monica said as she jumped up and grabbed a big flowered pot holder.

A feeling of nostalgia hit jack as he sat in the quaint little kitchen that had been his grandmothers for so long. Monica moved in last spring right after Granny had passed away. He felt like a little boy again sitting at that same old table waiting for something yummy to be presented from the oven. Monica had taken over the role in that little farm house almost as if granny was right there directing her. She even moved like Granny did and certainly made him feel as safe. Granny loved to bake and so did Monica. She had her own little bakery in town next to the general store.

Jack was deep in thought when he noticed Monica staring down at him. "What?" Was all she said.

"Oh nothing, just remembering Grams. You act just like her you know?" He said with a smile.

"Oh hush, I could never fill her shoes and you know it. She was a remarkable woman; hers would be some mighty big shoes to fill!" Monica stated as she turned back to examine her creations.

"You're probably right," he said, "you are way too mean to fill that sweet old lady's shoes!" he said with a grin right before he had to dodge the pot holder with big yellow daisies that had been their grandmothers.

"Ok buddy, now there's the Jack I know," she said as she filled his mouth with an enormous bite of pecan pie.

"Mmmm, good but very, very hot!" he mumbled and headed to the fridge to get a glass of milk.

"Well, that's what you get for picking on me little brother," she said as she wrapped him in a big bear hug.

"I think we are going to be alright," she said

"Jack just smiled at her and looked at the clock on the wall.

"Is that time right sis?" he asked.

"Yeah, why?" Monica replied.

Looking at his watch to double check he swallowed the last gulp of milk and said, "That's funny, bus must be running a little late today. Emily should have been here fifteen minutes ago."

"Probably just running a little late." She said, "She'll be here before we know it, and she can have a big ole piece of Granny's famous pecan pie while her daddy tells her she can quit fretting over all this non-sense of a missing ring."

Rolling his eyes he said, "You just think you know it all don't you Mon?"

"Of course I do, I'm your sister!" she said with a smile.

Just then Monica pulled her cell phone out of her jeans pocket. It had been on vibrate and she almost didn't notice it.

"Shit Jack!" She blurted.

"Hey Mon, didn't you just get on to me for cussing too much?" he asked.

"Well, read this and tell me what you think?" she said as she handed him her phone with a lengthy text from one of Emily's friend's mothers.

After reading it his only reply was, "Double shit!" as he grabbed both their jackets from the hook by the back door.

Monica took her jacket as she checked the oven to make sure it was off.

The drive to Wendi's house only took about five minutes but it felt like an eternity to both Jack and Monica.

Neither of them spoke a word as they flew through the small moss-covered town. Jack kept repeating what he had read over and over again in his frightened mind.

Wendi thought it was strange and had been shocked to hear the neighbor tell her that both girls were in the back yard in the tent. Becca hadn't asked to have a friend over and it was against her nature to do things without her mother's permission. When she found both little girls in the tent whispering about Emily running away from home she texted Monica as fast as she could. The little girls didn't know that she was outside the tent the whole time, but she was determined not to take her eyes off of it for a second.

Jack knew this was his fault but he couldn't keep the anger from his words when he and Monica jumped out of the truck and he ran across the yard to the tent and hurriedly unzipped the flap to find his daughter and her friend huddled close together.

"What is this I hear about you running away young lady?" Jack shouted.

Monica heard the whimpering start and couldn't' stand to let her little niece go through that alone. As she pushed a tense Jack out of her way she told Becca to go wait with her Mother. Monica then sat down next to Emily and combed her fingers through the child's tangled blond hair.

"Shhh baby, your daddy is just worried sick over this, he doesn't mean to yell." She cooed at Emily as she glared at Jack over the frightened girls head.

Jack gave a big 'Errrrrrrr' sound and then burst into tears as he too sat down on the other side of Emily.

Both Emily and Monica were startled by his response. Jack was a man who rarely cried. Emily had never seen her daddy cry and it had been so long since Monica had that she forgot he knew how. Jack hadn't even shed a tear at his Grandmother's funeral.

"I'm so sorry baby," jack blubbered, "you didn't do anything wrong, please don't ever leave daddy, I love you more than anything in the whole wide world." As Emily crawled in Jacks lap Monica put her arms around them both.

Jack got hold of his emotions and looked right at Emily as she too started wailing, "But you are mad at me, I don't deserve to live with you anymore, I'll run off and be a gypsy on the bayou."

Jack smiled hoping Emily wouldn't catch him. Ever since he had taken her to the county fair in August she had been talking about the fortune telling gypsies. "That won't be necessary princess, and don't ever let me hear you say you don't deserve to live with me, it is me that is honored to live with such a special little lady!" He said.

"I'm sorry I lost your ring Daddy, you can have all my allowance until it's paid off," she said.

"Honey it's just a ring, a thing, you are the real prize. Don't worry about it. But we are a team you and me, we have to stick together. Promise me you will always stay with daddy!"

Emily was so grown up in the next moments that Jack was afraid he was going to start crying again as she dried her eyes and looked up at him, took his face into both her little hands and said, "We are a team daddy, and we will always stick together."

Jack hugged them both and kissed Emily on her forehead.

"Let's go to Aunt Monica's and have some of her yummy pecan pies." He said as he stood up to stretch is weary legs and took Emily's hand into his.

Jack hadn't been sleeping well the past couple weeks and his body was definitely feeling the effects. He now realized that he had been worrying about all the wrong things. With his mind back on the important things in life he knew tonight would provide him with some much needed rest.

4

"Why do you want a job at The Dress Barn?" The pencil pushing little man behind the big oak desk asked her.

Angela wondered if he ever cracked a smile. She had been sitting in his sweltering office for over an hour. It certainly was not her idea of the ideal job, but since she dropped out of design school she didn't have many options. She had to go two counties over to find this little god-forsaken hole in the wall place, and now she was sitting here being interrogated by this pint sized pipsqueak in a power suit.

Angela groaned under her breath as she started to answer him.

"Oh, just forget it, you will do. You will sure look pretty at the registers," he said with a wink as he slowly eyed her up and down, making sure to spend extra time on her ample bosom. "And you can help those old bitties pick out their Sunday dresses. Shouldn't be too hard, surely a pretty little thing like you can figure that out."

Angela wanted to deck him. He must have thought he was being funny or flirtatious, but all she wanted to do was run screaming from his office to get as far away from him as she could. But, she sucked it up and thanked him for giving her the opportunity before she hurried out of there.

Driving home to Lacasine Angela wasn't surprised in the least to see that her little town had not changed much since she graduated high school three years ago. For a town with a population of less than one thousand it seemed to still be thriving. The parking lot was filled at the little general store/ice cream shop. She wondered if this was the last town on earth that still had a general store. Angela thought a chocolate malt would sure hit the spot after that sleazy man kept her in his sizzling office for so long. She slowed down but kept on driving as she passed the cheery little shop. She was not ready to run into anyone she knew just yet. While the chocolate sounded good a shower or two sounded better to get the creepy feeling her new boss had given her off her mind and body, so she headed down the next street to go on home.

As she was walking by Gretchen heard loud country music blaring from her daughter's bedroom. She quietly opened the door to peek in and found Angela in her bathrobe, hair a wet mess on top of her head with tears rolling down her face as she sat holding the bowl full of left over Halloween candy.

She walked in and sat down on the bed beside her daughter.

"Don't cry honey, you will find a job. We'll go out tomorrow and see what we can find." Gretchen consoled as she wiped the tears from her daughters face with a tissue off the night stand.

"Oh mom, I got the job." She blubbered.

"Then what is it sweetie?" Her mother asked.

"That man is horrible, just horrible!" She said.

"Who honey?" Gretchen asked with a confused look on her face.

"Mr. Montgomery, my new boss at the Dress Barn. He is such a creepy little man, but I'll just stay out of his way and do my job. I'll be fine." Angela sighed.

"Uh huh, so what's with the sugar fest you have going on here." Her mom said as she picked up a miniature chocolate bar.

"I found the leftover candy in the cabinet and decided eating it would be more lucrative then murdering my new boss before I even go in for my first day on the job." She said with a mouthful of nougat.

"Whatever you need to do honey, just remember you have to fit your little butt into all those pretty clothes we bought." She chimed.

Angela had always had a lovely figure. Gretchen was jealous. With her thin frame she knew she could never fill out her clothes like her daughter did hers.

Gretchen left her daughter to think and munch to the tune of 'Redneck Woman.'

"OMG Mom!, What is this?" Angela shouted from the doorway of the kitchen while Gretchen prepared a salad for the evening meal. She had decided to make a healthy supper since her daughter was having her dessert beforehand.

"What is what?" She said jumping back from the counter where she was slicing tomatoes.

"Sorry I scared you Mom, but look what was in the bowl of candy. Is this a joke?" She asked as she held up a beautiful diamond ring to see it sparkle as it caught the light from the sun streaming through the kitchen window.

"I don't know anything about it. Let's go ask your dad. Maybe he's trying to be sneaky." She said with a smile.

Angela and Gretchen found Ken working on his classic 68' cobalt blue Camaro in the garage. He had been tinkering with it for as long as Angela could remember. But, it kept him happy, and now that he was retired he could use all the happiness he could muster. For the first few months after retirement he spent his time in front of the television. Gretchen had been beside herself with worry that he was never going to break out of his slump.

Gretchen walked over to the creeper that he was lying on, put her hand on his leg and waited for him to surface.

Rolling out from under the pristine ride he raised his head up too soon and bumped it on the exhaust pipe before uttering a stream of words that weren't usually heard coming from his mouth.

"Sorry girls," He shyly said as he looked around and saw his wife and daughter staring back at him.

As Ken sat up his wife thrust a diamond ring at him.

"Well what do we have here?," he asked.

"You tell me honey," Gretchen said, "the candy bowl was not a good hiding place for an anniversary present if that's what you were thinking."

"Oh my Gretchen, I didn't have anything to do with this." He said.

With a guilty look on his face, He now knew he had better get her something good for their anniversary coming up just before Christmas.

"Well if not you then who Dad?" Angela asked as she took the ring from him to examine it again.

"You know, I think I remember something on a flyer at the grocery store," Her dad said.

"When were you at the grocery store?" Gretchen asked her husband.

With another guilty look he confessed that he had ran out of ice cream and potato chips.

"With the two of you eating like this I'm going to have to get the doors widened." Gretchen said.

Ignoring that comment Ken went on to tell them about a flyer that had been put up right after Halloween. A little girl was looking for a ring she had lost that belonged to her daddy.

"Well this sure isn't a man's ring!" Said Angela.

"Oh well, I guess we can put up our own flyer and put a notice in the paper. If someone lost it surely they will respond. If not I guess you have a lovely Anniversary gift that didn't cost me one red cent." Ken said to Gretchen.

"Oh honey, don't even try that. What you are going to get me will be way better than this, after that comment." She said with a devious smile as she snuggled up close to her husband and tried to hide her pinch to his hind quarters.

Angela pretended not to notice her parent's behavior as she said, "But you guys why would this ring be in our candy bowl if it doesn't belong to any of us?"

"Maybe your louse of an ex had someone sneak it into the Halloween candy when you were passing it out that night," her mom suggested.

"I seriously doubt it, mom, after the conversation we had on the phone before I left town he knows better than to try and show his face around me again," Angela said.

Angela left the ring in her parent's capable hands to do whatever they wanted with it after that. She was way too busy to be hunting down the owner of a missing ring. It was probably just a cheap ring from a child's Halloween costume. She thought to herself as she headed back into the house to decide what to wear on her first day at her new job.

— ~ —

"Uhgggggggggg." Was all Angela replied when she made it home from work the next evening when her mother asked her how it went.

"That doesn't tell me anything honey, are you happy, sad, indifferent?" Gretchen asked.

"Worn out!" She stated bluntly. "You would not believe how many elderly ladies came in today and needed help trying on clothes. I think I spent more time in the dressing rooms than anywhere else. I'm going to be lost when I have to work the registers by myself."

"Well, it sounds like you had productive day sweetie, and you are a fast learner, you will pick up the business side of it just like that!" Gretchen said snapping her fingers.

For as much as Angela couldn't stand her new boss she really loved the job. The week of orientation had flown by and she loved to help all the regulars especially now that it was the holiday season. Sweet little ladies called her by name and asked her advice on everything from what to buy their grandchildren for Christmas to what she thought of a suspicious mole they found while trying on clothes. For the first time in her adult life Angela felt like she was truly making a difference. She only had to put up with her creepy little boss on those rare occasions that he ventured out of his office. Angela was feeling like her life was falling back into place. She had received her first paycheck and although it was nowhere near what she was hoping to make working for a big design firm she felt good about the hard work she had done to earn the honest yet meager paycheck.

Angela had even begun to look up old friends on-line who she had known in High School, and was planning on meeting up with a couple of her girlfriends at Ricky's on Saturday night.

Ricky's was a karaoke bar about twenty miles away in Crowley. Her friend Denver had married Ricky right out of high school and they had opened the bar and had great success with it.

"Long time no see!" Denver greeted Angela as she cautiously strolled through the swinging doors made to look like an old time tavern.

"Great to see you!" Angela said sincerely as she grabbed her friends Denver and Chelsea in a big bear hug.

"Now don't get all emotional on us, it's not like any of us died, it's only been a few years!" Denver kidded as she wiped away the stray tear rolling down Angela's face.

"I know, but you guys don't know how good you look right now." She said as she pulled up a bar stool and sat down.

"Why thank you!" Both girls said in unison as they twirled around at the compliment.

"Oh hush with you, you know what I mean. It's been so long and it's so nice to see some familiar faces and have a night out to just blow off some steam." she said.

5

*J*ack sat back in the hardwood booth in the far corner of the bar nursing his beer while trying to listen to his friend as he chattered about the cost of a new juke box he was wanting to purchase for the bar.

"Hey you!" Ricky finally shouted after he realized Jack was somewhere lost in his own thoughts.

"Oh, man I'm sorry," Jack replied as he took a long swig and sighed as he sat back and put his arm up on the back of the booth not noticing when he bumped the girl sitting behind him.

"Dude liven up." Ricky said, "I've been trying to get you out of your funk for almost two weeks now. Tonight I'm going to get you wasted and put your ass up there on that stage. You are going to sing your heart out until you forget about whatever the hell it is that is bothering you, if I have to keep the bar open until dawn."

"Two beers is the limit man, I have to drive home and be up early tomorrow. And I am fine." Jack said in a huff.

"Heeeeeey Cowboy!" Jack heard the shrill voice in his right ear coming from a familiar looking brunette as she and another female both plopped down on opposite sides of him.

"Why are you abusing my girl, huh feller?" Denver asked again in the same loud obnoxious shrill voice.

"Stop it Denver! You are drunk!" said Ricky

Jack pushed away the hand with the long fingernail that was repeatedly being poked in his chest.

"What are you talking about? I'm not abusing anyone." Jack said as he glanced to his left and looked into the dark eyes of the pretty blond sitting silently next to him.

"Yes you are, you hit my dear friend, Angela, here on the head with your bony elbow and I think she deserves an apology. She was our prom queen and is a big fashion designer now. Show some respect buddy!" She said loudly as she started poking him with her long fingernail again.

"Geez Denver, just because you have the night off does not mean you need to drink all the profit!" Ricky said as he pulled his wife up by the arm and sat her down on his side of the booth.

"You smell like a still, woman! What have you been drinking?" He asked.

'None of your business," Denver said jumping back up and puling on Jacks arm telling him he was going to have to sing Karaoke since he hit Angela on the head.

Jack decided not to argue with a drunken lady so he jumped up and grabbed Angela's hand as he went.

"Alright, but if I sing so does the prom queen." he said with a wink at Angela

"I'm not a prom queen anymore, cowboy!" Angela replied as she downed the rest of her Lemon Drop.

Angela and Jack were both nervous standing in front of the sparsely filled smoky bar preparing to sing the song Denver had picked out for them.

"Why do you guys keep calling me cowboy?" Jack whispered.

Angela simply smiled and pointed to the big black Stetson sitting atop his head.

"Oh," he blushed, "I guess I didn't take that off after work."

The song was starting before Angela could ask where he worked.

Angela and Jack rushed back to the booth before Denver could make them stay for an encore.

"Friends in Low Places' is certainly fitting for her tonight." Jack said pointing to Denver as Ricky was helping her to the bathroom.

"I'm sorry about that, I haven't seen her in so long, I think she just overdid it tonight." Angela apologized.

"Don't worry about it. I had fun." He replied with a half-smile.

"Are you sure? You look pretty stressed." Angela inquired.

"I'm sorry, just a lot going on with my little girl right now." He said hoping giving out that information wouldn't be a red flag for her. It had been a very long time since Jack felt such an instant attraction to a woman.

"Oh, you have a little girl? What is her name?" she asked, hoping he wasn't married or involved.

What am I thinking? She thought to herself. *A little girl needs a mother. Why am I being a jerk hoping that he is a single dad?*

"Her name is Emily. She's six years old and the light of my life." He said.

After a long pause he started again, "Her mother left us when she was just two months old. Actually I didn't even know about her until she was two months old."

"I'm sorry, that must have been hard on you." Angela sympathized

"Well, it has definitely been challenging, that's for sure. But I love that little girl with my whole heart. She has me wrapped around her finger. I'm afraid I have been hard on her lately. I guess that's what I am doing here tonight, trying to drown my sorrows." He said before adding, "I don't know why I am unloading on you. You were just out for the night with your friend and got dumped on this Cowboy."

Angela laughed nervously as he pointed to his Cowboy hat to try and lighten the mood.

"Well it was supposed to be a girls night out, but our other friend Chelsea left after about an hour and that's when Denver started downing the shots like she thought they would run out or something."

As they sat there talking the hours flew by. Angela told him the story of being Prom Queen only by process of elimination after the only two girls running had come down with the flu on the night of Prom. Then she told him the story of how she had gone to school to be a designer, but had to drop out because of a bad relationship and had decided to move back home.

Jack told Angela a little about his college days and how he now worked as a field guide for the lodge down on the bayou showing tourists how to hunt Alligators and Nutria.

Before either of them knew it the bartender called last call as the song 'Closing Time' came on.

"Whoa, where did the time go?" Angela asked as she looked at the table and saw that she had drank three more Lemon drops and a shot of something apparently, since there was an empty shot glass sitting in front of her.

It was then that she felt it all hit her and realized that she couldn't possibly drive home.

"Are you ok, you just turned white as a sheet?" Jack said eyeing her cautiously hoping she was not going to need help to the bathroom like her friend had.

"I'm okaaaaayyyy." She slurred right before she passed out.

$\sim$ $\sim$

"Jack what are you doing bringing a girl home!" Monica chastised her younger brother.

"What the hell was I supposed to do with her Mon, she passed out at the bar, I couldn't very well leave her there. Can you drive her to her car when she wakes up and try not to let Emily see her." He pleaded.

Monica had been staying with Jack and Emily since Emily had tried to run away. Jack had been beside himself with worry and Monica knew he would feel better with her there for a few days, whether he admitted it or not. She had to use the excuse that she was the one who was frightened to get him to let her stay and dote on her little brother and niece.

Monica just scowled at him as he left through the back door to head to the lodge that morning. She didn't even think to ask what the woman's name was, and she began to wonder if he even knew it. For all they knew she could be casing the place and had plans to make out with all their stuff.

"Well I'll be damned if that happens!" She muttered to herself as she got up to fix Emily's breakfast before waking her to get ready for school.

"Aunt Monica," Emily whispered as she slid her little hand against Monica's bare knee sticking out from under her green flannel gown. Monica jumped at the touch from her little niece causing both girls to scream.

"I'm sorry honey, you scared Aunt Mon. What are you doing up so early?" She asked.

"I heard a loud noise coming from Daddy's room and when I peeked in you won't believe what I saw." She said in a rush as her eyes got big as the Silver Dollar pancakes her aunt was cooking up for the morning meal. Monica didn't want to have to be the one to explain a strange woman in the house but it seemed inevitable at this point.

"Well, Aunt Monica, don't you want to know, huh, huh, huh?" Emily said while bouncing around the kitchen table.

"Let me explain honey," she started before being interrupted by the excited child.

"There's an angel in there, I saw her wings and halo. She's so pretty. I bet she's here because I prayed for daddy to meet an angel to be my new Mommy." She said with enthusiasm in her voice.

"Oh sweetie, that's not an angel, it's just a lady who----" she started again before being interrupted by her niece once more.

Emily sat the glass of milk she had just poured down on the table with a large splash falling onto the red checkered placemats as she grabbed her Aunts hand and pulled hard to get her to follow her.

"Come on Aunt Mon, look and see!"

"I guess its truth time," Monica said quietly to herself as Emily pulled her reluctantly down the hallway toward Jacks bedroom.

"What's that Aunt mon?" Emily asked.

"Oh nothing honey." She said while patting her nieces head as they stood before the closed door.

— ~

"Where the heck am I." Angela said aloud to herself as she sat up and looked around what was sure to be a room belonging to a man.

Her head was pounding from the drinks she had the night before and she was sure she had made a terrible mistake waking up in a room that she did not recognize. She groaned loudly as she threw herself back against the mattress while pulling the white fluffy blanket over her head. She didn't even look to see what she knocked off the headboard that caused such a loud crash.

Monica didn't realize she was holding her breath until she exhaled loudly as she slowly opened the door to her brother's bedroom. With his clothes strewn about and towels hanging from the burlap lamp shade and even a pair of boxers hanging from the antlers of the big buck he had shot when he went to visit his college roommate in his hometown in Missouri, Monica was sure Jack hadn't been completely honest with her about what went on the previous night.

"Look Monica, just look, it's an angel. I see her fluffy wings and golden halo. Oh, it's just what I had prayed for. God sent daddy an angel!" Emily exclaimed.

Startled at the voices in the room Angela sat up like a lightning bolt had hit her.

"Oh my goodness, I can't believe it!" Cried Monica, "that's not an angel, that's little Angela Baker!"

"Who are you, and where am I at?" Angela asked while peeking under the covers to make sure she was still fully dressed.

"Don't you remember me? Well of course not, you were just in kindergarten when I was a teacher's aide and helped out in your art class." Monica explained, " I'm Miss Murphy, or Monica to you now that you are all grown."

"She's not an angel." Sighed Emily as she turned and went back down the hallway with her Aunt hot on her trail.

"Be right back." Monica shouted over her shoulder for Angela's benefit.

Back in the kitchen with Emily only a few steps ahead of her, Monica found her niece already eating pancakes that she had snagged from the big platter Monica had sitting on the stove.

"Want to talk about it," Monica asked.

"No!" Emily screeched.

"I will try to explain sweetie." She consoled while rubbing her nieces shoulders.

Throwing her hands in the air Emily burst into tears and started blubbering about the angel wings and yellow halo. She was sobbing and shuttering so hard that Monica couldn't make it all out.

Sitting beside her she pulled the crying child into her lap.

"I really thought she was an an an angel," she stammered.

"Why did you think that honey?" she asked

"Because that is what I prayed for and then I saw her with the white fluffy blanket around her and her hair was sticking out. She looked like an angel." she explained.

"Daddy has been so lonely and so mad lately, he needs an angel to be my new mommy so he won't have to worry so much about me." she wailed again while hiding her face in her aunts nightgown.

"Oh honey, you and your daddy will be just fine. When the time is right God will send you and your daddy a nice lady.

"Uh, sorry to interrupt." Angela said from the kitchen doorway.

Monica and Emily looked up at the same time to see her standing there in her low slung jeans, brown cowboy boots and white blouse she had on from the night before.

She felt very vulnerable waiting there for their evaluation of her presence.

Monica sat Emily down in her own chair and told her to finish her breakfast while she took Angela into the living room to talk to her.

—　—

Angela felt out of it all day at work. Luckily she hadn't worked the day before so no one at work was suspicious of her wearing the same clothes two days in a row. She felt better after having talked to Monica. She vaguely remembered her from elementary school and was extremely embarrassed about the whole situation with Jack. She was relieved to find out that he had only taken her home because she had passed out before she could tell him where she lived. Monica re-assurred her that Jack was a good upstanding man who would never take advatage of a woman. Somehow she already knew that. The night before was still a little blurry to her, but she had a good feeling about Jack. She only hoped he didn't think she was a bar hopping lush who couldn't hold her liquor. She felt she would be lucky if he ever spoke to her again after the great first impression she had made.

Her mother and father eyed her suspiciously when she finally returned home after work that evening, but neither one questioned her whereabouts the night before. She was always grateful to have such trusting parents. It seemed they were more laid back and relaxed than her friends parents had been. She always thought she was just more mature and they realized that, but after thinking back on the recent events of her life, she wasn't so sure. Sometimes she had felt her parents put too much trust in her. Growing up she knew she could always count on them if things got too tough or if she was in a bind, but she was really given a lot of freedom to stand on her own two feet and make responsible choices. Angela figured this was due to her parents having her so late in life. They were calmer and more laid back by the time she arrived. Her Dad was nearing seventy and her mother was now sixty-two. Whatever their reasoning was to have so much trust in her judgement she was grateful this week. Neither of them said a word about her being out overnight. Her Mother did give her a worried look or two and asked her if everything was alright, but in the end no one said 'boo' and for that she was truly grateful. She felt bad enough on her own without someone else putting their two cents in. She knew she would be humiliated if she ever ran into Jack or his sister again.

6

"Of I'm going down that Bitch is going down with me!" mumbled Dewer Looking around the gray, drab interrogation room he refused to make eye contact with the prick who was trying to get answers from him.

"That's not what I asked you!" said the DA loudly as he slammed his black leather briefcase down hard on the dusty table.

"Just who the hell are you talking about?" he asked rising to his feet.

The officer started to move causing the DA to gain perspective of where he was and he sat back down again.

"Answer his question!" The officer said

"Angela, yeah, Angela, it was all her idea. She made me do it." he snorted and coughed into his hand.

"Just who is this Angela man?" the DA questioned. He had been tailing this guy for two years now. There was never evidence of a female in the mix. He knew his reputation was riding on bringing this dirt bag in and he planned on doing so very quickly.

— ~ —

"This is not a drill people!" Cried Mr Mongomery as he paced back and forth behind the three cashiers at the registers and the four women who were strategically spread across the floor at the Dress Barn. "It's almost Thanksgiving and Christmas is just around the corner. We are going to sell, sell, and sell. Time is money. Don't let anyone leave empty handed. Sell like your life depends on it!"

Angela tuned him out as he droned on and on. She could already see the ladies lined up outside the front door. It was nice to see some familiar faces that looked genuinely happy to see her there. Of course with her nosey little boss lurking around she wouldn't be able to visit with them like she was used to doing.

The day flew by. Angela was making sales left and right and had even found time to catch up on the gossip from the Red Hat Ladies and the Silver Shoes Society. Amazingly she had discovered that she loved coming to work every day to see these sweet ladies who had become her friends. One particularly chatty lady was bending her ear when her boss stormed by and told her that if she wanted to gossip with the old bitties she needed to take a job in the hair salon.

He said it loud enough that three of the regulars dropped what they were looking at and left the store. Mrs. Adams, who she had been talking to, had already made her purchases, but she too stopped talking, grabbed her many bags and left the store with tears in her eyes She squeezed Angela's hand and gave her a half smile before she left.

"That's it!" Mr. Montgomery shouted, "Am I going to have to make an example of you? We are not here to visit. We are here to make sales! Just who do you--------"

Clutching his chest he stopped in mid-sentence.

Gasping he fell to the floor at her feet.

The two other cashiers became hysterical at the sight before them. Both drew in a sharp breath and let out a shrill yelp.

Angela remembered CPR from her High School Health class and immediately dropped to the floor in her dress and heels to check his pulse and see if he was breathing.

She'd been doing CPR for nearly half an hour when the paramedics finally arrived. With sweat running down her neck and into the deep crevices her designer dress was no longer properly concealing she stood up and wiped the moisture from her brow. For as disheveled as she looked and as tired as she felt she was feeling good about the whole situation when her boss was stabilized and rolled away on the gurney. She'd make a point to call his wife and go visit him in the hospital tomorrow after work. Her co-workers were stunned into silence and looking at her with awe.

"Sorry." Was all her young coworker uttered as she laid a sympathetic hand on Angela's arm. The young girl had called 911 for Angela after she had to practically shout to get her to quit her hysterics and pay attention to the situation at hand. After getting the girl to call 911 she was not able to get her to help her with CPR. Her and Angela's other co-workers had stood back while Angela took the reins and went it alone.

She just smiled at her co-workers as she picked up her purse and keys from the break room and started to head for the door toward her car. She was sure not in the mood to go back to work and was certain no one would make a fuss about her leaving a couple hours early.

The afternoon sun was particularly warm on that November afternoon as she made her way across the shopping center parking lot.

Limping along on her broken heel while trying to pull her torn skirt down over her knees she didn't notice the black Chevy pickup that pulled up beside her or the tall man who had gotten out of it and was now walking toward her.

"Angela?" Jack questioned as he gently tapped her on the shoulder.

She lost her balance on the one good heel and would have fallen if it hadn't been for jack's strong arms catching her.

"Whoa, girl! It's been a long time since I had a woman fall for me like that!" He teased as he helped her to steady herself.

I seriously doubt that. She thought to herself as she eyed the denim clad hunk standing beside her.

"What happened to you?" He asked waving his hand up and down in front of her disheveled attire, with hair falling into her eyes, and sweat making her open blouse cling to her in places Jack didn't dare focus on here in a public place.

Angela tried to put some semblance back into her hair and what used to be a nice outfit as she blew out a deep breath she had been holding and said, "very long day!"

"Want to tell me about it?" He asked

Avoiding his question Angela asked one in return, "How did you find me?"

"Well," Jack began as he thought about telling her he had been waiting outside The Dress Barn every night for the past three nights in hopes to get to "run into her." His sister had told him where she worked the day she had driven Angela back to her car and Jack had been trying to accidentally on purpose run into her ever since.

"I was just thinking of doing some early Christmas shopping and saw you heading to your car." He lied.

"Oh, well I'm sorry I look like this," she said, "My boss gave us quite a scare this afternoon."

"Did he attack you or something?" He asked with concern in his voice.

"No, no nothing like that." She said with a wave of her hand. "I'm so tired, I just want to go home and forget about it."

"How bout we sit down over there under the shade tree and I'll get us some sweet teas and we can talk about it?" He asked, hopeful she wouldn't just turn tail and leave after he had finally gotten up the courage to approach her.

Hesitating Angela said, "Alright, but I am not going shopping with you, I couldn't go into a store looking like this!"

"You look beautiful Ma'am." Jack said with a smile as he waited for Angela to put on the sneakers she had in her back seat and slam the door shut

Against her better judgment Angela did go shopping with Jack. She had such a good time talking with him under that big oak tree outside the shopping center that she didn't want their "date" to end when he said he had better get to the toy store before it closed.

Both of them found it very easy to talk with one another. Angela told Jack her harrowing tale of the scare with her boss, and Jack told her about his day at the lodge. After she helped him pick out some Christmas presents for his daughter at the toy store they decided to have some pasta at the diner next to it.

Angela was surprised to look at her watch and see that she had been enjoying herself so much that the afternoon had gotten away from her. It was after eight when her and Jack made their way to their vehicles.

"Looks like you didn't get to go home and get that extra rest you were hoping for." He said as he fidgeted with his keys beside her door.

"That's ok. You kept me company and I had a nice time. I just hope Emily will like the things we picked out." she answered.

"I'm sure she will. You know what little girls like more than I do. I would have been lost without you." He said with a smile.

"I'm sure you would have done just fine and she would love anything given to her by her father." She said, not really thinking about what she was saying, but rather focusing on the soft lips of this man who was quickly getting under her skin. She loved the way he looked in the moonlight and was just wondering if he was going to kiss her goodnight when he leaned down and placed a light kiss across her hungry mouth.

"Do you have plans for Thanksgiving?" Angela asked when she once again could catch her breath.

"Yeah, my sister is going to cook a big meal on Saturday at my folk's house. Mom and dad will be out of town and Mon has to work on Thanksgiving." He said.

"Well, if you and Emily want to you can come to my house. Mom loves to cook and I'm sure there will be plenty. She will have a heyday with extra bodies to fuss over."

— —

Angela felt bad that Frank, her boss whose first name she was just now learning, had to spend Thanksgiving in the hospital. But he looked good. Angela and her friend Denver went to visit him after she got off work the next afternoon. He and his wife couldn't thank her enough for her quick actions that ultimately saved his life. Frank had a bad heart and ended up having to have a triple bypass. He was recovering and his prognosis was good she was told.

"I thought you couldn't stand him?" Denver said as they were leaving the hospital.

"I can't at work, but I couldn't just let him lie there and die when he collapsed in front of me." Angela answered. "Besides, he's not so bad when his wife is around. Did you see them together? They were so sweet. That's what I want. Did you see how his eyes lit up every time he looked at her?" Angela found herself daydreaming of Jack and the kiss they has shared in the moonlight the night before.

"All I saw was how she jumped up at every command that came out of his mouth. 'Get me water.' 'fluff my pillow.' ehhhhh, sickening Angela, you really thought that was sweet?"

"Denver, he just had a heart attack and major surgery. Didn't you see him clinging to her and holding her hand, caressing her hair? He's grateful to be alive." She replied.

"Whatever, he's just like any other man, always demanding something." she scoffed.

"What has gotten into you?" Angela asked. "Are things ok with you and Ricky?"

Denver got quiet and looked out the passenger's window as Angela was pulling out of the hospital parking lot.

"Are you going to talk to me? She urged.

"What's there to say, we just aren't happy anymore. It's all work and no fun anymore. He's always in a bad mood about that stupid bar. He's more worried about it than he ever is about me or the kids. I don't even think he knows we exist. I can't remember the last time he just talked to me or kissed me. You know I had to take the kids camping all by myself this past summer. He said he was too busy to even get away for a couple days, and he tried to make me feel bad for wanting to go. You know he had a little girl when we got married right? Well she is almost seven now and loves to camp. And so does our three year old. He wanted me to take them to my mom's so I could stay and help him run the bar. Sometimes I think I can't do it anymore." She blurted in one quick huff.

"I'm sorry Denver, I didn't know you guys were having such a hard time." she said

"Well, how could you! You left and went to New York to live the high life while the rest of us stayed here to rot." she cried.

"Whoa, that's enough of that." Angela said with a grimace. "You could have gone to college anywhere you wanted. You graduated with honors. You are the one who decided to get married and start a family right away."

They had only made it down a couple streets when Angela decided to turn the car around and take her friend to the playground behind their old elementary school. Growing up whenever either of them was having a hard time they would go play on the swings until they could wrap their minds around whatever it was that was causing them trouble.

"What are you doing Ang? We aren't kids anymore. This is real life. I didn't get a bad grade, I have a bad marriage. You can't fix that by playing on the playground.

Ignoring her Angela parked the car and got out.

The two of them swung and talked like they were teenagers again. When Angela got Denver to open up it was like a flood gate.

Driving home that night Angela was feeling like she had found her long lost friend. Denver apologized for snapping at her and they both shared the hardships they were going through. The girls decided never to go for so long without talking ever again. Whether they ever really solved anything or not they both realized they felt better having a friend to confide in.

"You sure look chipper." Her Mother remarked as Angela kicked off her shoes at the door and hung her bag on the hook.

Sinking down into the big recliner in the living room felt heavenly. "I spent the afternoon with Denver, Mom, she needed a shoulder to cry on." She said.

"I'm glad you were there for her honey." Gretchen whispered in her daughter's ear as she kissed her cheek. "Did you see your boss?"

"Yeah, she went with me to visit him in the hospital. He is going to be fine. I don't think he will be working anytime soon, though." She answered.

"That's my baby girl, always looking out for everyone else. I'm so proud of the woman you have become. " She said smiling proudly at her daughter.

"Oh mom, I think you are forgetting I just had to run home with my tail between my legs a few weeks ago." She sighed.

"Yes, but you are bouncing back and I am happy to see you moving on with your life instead of letting a little set-back get you down and keep you there." She said.

"Mom, quitting school just before the final semester of my senior year is not just a 'little set-back.'" Angela argued.

"You and Daddy are so great, you don't even know the half of it, and you took me back with open arms."

"That's what parents are for sweetie. Unconditional love comes with the territory. I know we raised you right and you will do right for it. You have a good head on your shoulders." She said.

About that time Ken came running in the house almost out of breath holding a large yellow envelope in front of him, and thrust it at Angela.

"I almost forgot about this. It was delivered two days ago." he said when he caught his breath.

"What is it Daddy?" Angela asked turning the large envelope over in her hands.

"Certified letter to Ms. Angela Baker. Oh my!" She exclaimed.

Slowly she opened the envelope to find a court order with the first line being, 'The State of New York vs. Dewer Grant and Angela Baker.'

7

"Guess what Aunt Monica?" Said Emily when her Aunt dropped her friend off at her house after the girls had been playing on the playground that afternoon.

"What honey?" She asked as she looked in the rearview before backing out of the drive.

"I saw Daddy's angel again!" she said beaming.

"What are you talking about?" she asked.

"That lady who I thought was an angel but she really wasn't; well now I know she is." She said in a rush.

"Oh you do, do you?" Monica questioned

"Yeah, Yeah, she was swinging on the swings with just a regular girl, but she had the prettiest angel hair and when she swung back I could see in the sun light it looked just like a halo!" She said. "I didn't talk to her but I know she's daddy's angel, even if you don't believe me Aunt Mon. I just know it!"

Monica knew from her morning chat with Jack that he had spent the last couple nights talking on the phone with this so-called angel until the wee hours of the morning. Jack looked as if he could barely keep his eyes open this morning. But she did notice a calmness to him that hadn't been there in quite some time. While she was fond of little

Angela Baker, and she seemed to have grown up to be a good woman despite their first encounter in Jacks bedroom, Monica was skeptical of Emily putting her on such a high pedestal. She didn't want her little niece to get her feelings hurt once again. Just because her baby brother had been chatting with this woman and had been on a couple un-official dates she knew he kept the walls up around his heart when it came to dating. He was afraid to let anyone get too close for fear Emily would get hurt. She smiled at Emily as she pulled into her brother's driveway.

"You really have been great through all this." Angela said to Jack as they sat at the bar in her mother's kitchen digesting their Thanksgiving meal.

"Putting his hands on hers Jack looked into her eyes and said, "I enjoy my time with you."

Blushing she tried her best to think of something to say that didn't have to do with courts or lawyers or ex boyfriends. She had been so mad the past two days she could spit fire. The day after she received her court summons she had gone into Baton Rouge to find a lawyer. With her mother and father by her side she had to tell the lawyer the whole story about falling for the loser who made her believe he worked for Gucci. She had to tell how she moved him into her apartment and all the places they had gone, weekend excursions, everything they had bought, right down to what they ate. She was mortified to have her parents find out she had been living with Evan, or Dewar.

The lawyer told them what he was able to find out about the case. Apparently Dewar had been using fake and stolen ID's for years. He would run up charges on credit cards that he obtained under a false identity and of course skip out on the bills. He had up to twenty aliases that he had gone by in the course of the few short years. He had been doing this all over the US and parts of Canada. Angela had to give him a little credit; he did live in Paris just before he moved to New York, so he didn't lie to her about that...just everything else. The lawyer said that the police there had caught on to his act rather quickly and he fled to

New York in hopes of blending in, in such a large city. Angela unfortunately had been the beneficiary of him trying to lay low for a little while. He had talked her into using her frequent flyer miles and even charging some meals and other things on her account. Her lawyer told her he thought this was just to throw her off. If she only suspected him of just being a creep who made his girlfriend pay for everything then maybe she wouldn't suspect him for the creep he actually was. What she didn't know was that he had stolen a couple of her friends ID's and had made ID's with her picture on them, thus dragging her into his little scheme.

Angela was drained of all energy after leaving the lawyers office early that afternoon. After hours of discussion and telling him her side of the story she was assured that all charges against her would have to be dropped. They still had to go to court in January and plead her case, and they still had to convince the judge that she was in no way involved in the on-going conspiracy that she had been innocently dragged into. Angela felt like a fool. She felt lower than low and couldn't bring herself to face her parents for the remainder of the day.

For some reason she had even felt worse confessing her story to Jack. He had been very understanding and even had her laughing when they hung up the phone at one AM on Thanksgiving morning. That was just what she needed to conjure up the energy to get up and help her mother prepare the Thanksgiving meal.

She was lost in her thoughts and didn't realize he was still holding her hands until her gave a squeeze that brought her back to the present.

"A penny for your thoughts." Jack said smiling at her.

"Oh buddy, you don't want to know my thoughts right now." she said.

"I'm sorry, just too much going on to process." She said as she pulled her hands away and picked up both their empty coffee cups.

"Want so more?" she asked.

"Just more of this," He said taking the coffee cups and sitting them aside as he took both her hands in his again.

"I know we don't know each other too well yet, but this feels right, don't you think?"

Looking at her with hope in his dark brown eyes he hoped he hadn't said too much too fast to scare her away.

"It does." Was all she could say before her mother pranced into the kitchen arms loaded with dirty dishes.

Jumping up Angela said, "Here mom, let me help you."

"No, ma'am, you were up before I was this morning, baking away. Let me take care of the cleanup and you two go out and enjoy the stars on that old swing on the back porch. It sure is a nice night. Get some fresh air and let your old ma feel useful again!"

Jumping up from her seat at the bar she held out her elbow to Jack and said teasingly, "Shall we kind sir?"

Without hesitation Jack entwined his arm with hers as she led the way to the door.

As she walked by her mother Angela kissed her on the cheek and whispered, "thank you."

Gretchen just smiled and went about her business putting mashed potatoes and vegetables in containers to refrigerate.

The night air was cool on his face as he watched hers light up in the moonlight. He loved how she kept pushing the loose strands away from the soft skin on her exposed neck. Jack was wondering if what his daughter had been saying was true. Was this his angel? He had certainly become quite smitten with he and he was determined to share a few more kisses over the course of the evening to help him make his determination.

Angela and Jack were curled together under a chambray throw she had found on the back of the porch swing, both sound asleep when Emily tiptoed up to them and then said loudly, "Wake up!"

In a daze they both sat up abruptly. Jack quickly pushed the throw they had shared over onto Angela's lap as he took his daughter into his big arms and said, "what's the big idea little lady?"

Emily giggled, "You two sleepy heads fell asleep when Ken and I went for a drive in his car!"

"Just a pretend drive.....right honey?" Jack asked as he looked to Angela for reassurance.

Ken had been listening at the door since he was the one to find his daughter and Jack asleep. He and Emily had thought it would be funny to see how close she could get before they woke up.

Chuckling he made his presence known as he lumbered out onto the back porch.

"Dad, what's this I hear of you taking that car out for a drive? I thought it wasn't ready yet?" Angela scolded.

As Emily ran to his side he patted her on the head and said, "Jacks got himself a fine little girl here. She and I worked real hard after supper and finished putting that last belt on. We took that old beauty down the street and around the block. Runs like a charm!"

Ken was beaming. Angela was a little upset that she didn't get to go with her dad for the test drive, but she was happy that he and Emily had made a connection. He was a great father, always patient and understanding, and she knew that someday he would be a wonderful grandfather as she watched and listened to him and Emily tell their tale of the cars maiden voyage.

When the four of them made their way back into the house Ken excused himself and went to the living room to find his wife asleep in his big recliner. "Like Mother like Daughter." He said.

Standing in the kitchen Jack looked at his watch in disbelief. Again he had spent hours with this woman and he hadn't even realized it. It was well past ten o'clock when he announced that it was time to get Emily home and into bed.

"Ah Daddy, I'm having such a good time. Can't we stay longer?" She pleaded as she made her way toward Angela. I didn't even get to see the pretty Angels room or all her Angel clothes."

"Another time princess." Jack said as he turned to direct her out to the truck. Out of the corner of his eye Jack spotted something that looked familiar. Something shiny was sitting in a glass vase behind the kitchen sink. As he made his way closer to get a better look he thought his heart had stopped.

Emily noticed her daddy tense up and hurried to his side.

"What is wrong Daddy?" She asked.

In barely a whisper Jack said, "Go to the living room."

"Why Daddy, I thought we were leaving." She said.

Louder this time and with more fierceness than she had seen in him in a while he said, "Now!"

When Emily was safely out of ear shot Jack turned to Angela pointing at the ring, "What the Hell are you doing with my ring?"

Confused at the question Angela asked, "What ring/"

Jack took a step toward the glass vase and reached his hand into it to retrieve the ring he thought was gone forever.

"This ring, where did you get this ring?!?" he said, "Did you steal my ring and then play nice to me to get into my life? Are you working for Mystique?"

He was visibly shaking by this point and Angela was more than a little afraid of what she was witnessing. She knew a little of Mystique from their conversations, but she certainly didn't know her personally.

Confused she said, "Tell me what you are talking about?"

As she reached for his hand he quickly stepped away from her causing her even more confusion.

"That was a ring we found in the Halloween bucket after the kids had come trick-or-treating. I didn't even know it was still here. My Mom and Dad were supposed to take care of it." She tried to explain her very little knowledge of the ring he was waving around like a mad man.

With wild eyes Jack looked at her. He wanted to believe this beautiful woman he was quickly falling for. He was beginning to feel so comfortable with her that it scared him. He hadn't felt such a connection with anyone since Mystique was in his life and if he was being completely honest with himself there was an ever deeper connection with the woman who was standing before him with fear in her eyes. They had spent hours on the phone telling each other of their hopes and dreams. They had had long discussions about their families and their childhood memories. He now felt like a fool having poured his heart out to someone who may be in cahoots with his ex. He couldn't risk anything or anyone getting in between him and his daughter.

"I've got to go, we've got to go, I can't stay here." He stammered as he made his way toward the living room where Emily was waiting.

Pleading with him Angela said, "Jack no, please stay, you can't possibly think I stole your ring or want any harm to come to you or your daughter!"

Walking away he said, "I don't know what to think anymore."

Jack found Emily sitting in the living room with Ken playing checkers.

"Come Now!" he said as he kept walking without looking back.

"Jack!" Angela called as she followed him from the kitchen trying to keep up with his quick strides.

Jack was out the door and had the truck started when she turned toward Emily who was just getting up from the old card table where the checker board was set up. Angela gave her a half smile and said, "Tell him to call me."

Passing her mother in the hallway while she quickly made her way to her bedroom Angela burst out in tears.

"What is it honey?" she asked.

"Didn't you think it was a successful meal? Your boyfriend sure has a big appetite and his little girl is adorable. I think your Daddy likes her awful well."

"Oh mom, it's not that, the meal was wonderful, you did a great job hosting, as usual. It's just Jack, who isn't my boyfriend, I don't even think he wants to be my friend anymore after tonight." She said sobbing on her mother's shoulder as she led her into the bathroom to dry her eyes.

"Now don't say that, he seemed to be having a lovely time." she replied.

Looking up at her mother Angela told her that the ring they had found belonged to Jack and had apparently been one he had given his ex-fiancé, Emily's mother.

"Honey, I'm so sorry, your Daddy said he was going to get the number off that flyer the next time he was at the grocery store and we just put it in that old vase so we wouldn't forget." Gretchen said with shock in her voice.

"Great mom!, Now it's been weeks and he thinks I stole it from him!" She blubbered as the tears started again.

Angela ran from the bathroom and threw herself on her pink bedspread atop the twin sized bed in her little room.

8

"What did you do!?!" Shouted Monica as she threw open Jacks bedroom door not bothering to knock.

Jack was sitting at his desk with his head in his hands. "I don't want to talk about it!" he said without looking up.

Monica crossed the room in a huff and stood beside her little brother with her arms crossed.

"Well we're going to talk about it!" She said, "Emily is out there crying her little eyes out. She told me that you ruined things with her Angel. What gives Jack?"

Pulling his hands away from his face he slammed them down on the desk and said, "I told you I am not talking about it!"

"Come on little brother. From the look on your face and how you've been floating around here this past week I could swear you were falling in love with that girl." She said in a calmer voice.

'You aren't going to give up are you?" he said rising from his chair. Jack put his hand in his pocket and pulled out the ring and handed it to Monica.

"Oh my," she gasped, "Are you proposing to her? Did she say no? Is that what's wrong?"

"Hell no Monica, I am not rushing into anything ever again. That is the ring Emily took from my drawer and wore with her Halloween costume. For some reason Angela ended up with it!"

"Why did she have it?" She looked confused.

"I don't know, she said she found it. For all I know she is friends with Mystique and they are trying to take Emily from me." He said.

"Shhhhh, be quiet, the door is open!" Monica said as she hurried to shut the door to keep her little Niece from hearing this conversation.

"Now Jack, does that sound reasonable? Why would she want your ring and how the devil do you propose that would help Mystique get Emily back?" She asked in a voice that reminded him of his late Grandmother.

"Geez Mon, I don't have all the facts, but she sure isn't who I thought she was if she's been hiding this ring from me?" he said as he sat hard on his bed and picked up his old wrestling trophy to twirl around on his hands like he often did when he was nervous.

Monica left Jack alone with his thoughts as she made her way back to the kitchen to find Emily chowing down on the leftover chocolate chip cookies they had made the night before.

"Hey sweetheart can your old Aunt join you?" Monica said as she sat down beside Emily at the Kitchen table.

"Aunt Mon, why is Daddy mad at that Angel? We had so much fun at her house today. She's so nice she let me help her serve the pies and her Daddy let me help fix his fancy car and ride in it. I wish daddy would stop being mad." She said looking up at Monica with a milk mustache and cookie crumbs on her little face.

Monica's heart went out to her. Since there was no convincing her that Angela was not a real angel she didn't bother arguing that point with her.

"Your daddy is just confused right now sweetie. He'll cool off tomorrow and be right as rain when we all go see Grams and Gramps for Thanksgiving dinner on Saturday." She said hoping she was right.

"What are you doing here man, the lodge is closed until Monday." said Ricky as he walked into the tack room to find his friend cleaning the horse stalls.

Ricky worked at the lodge in the mornings before going into the bar. He liked having the quiet time to himself and wasn't expecting to find Jack invading his space that morning.

"Just blowing off steam." He said without looking up as he continued raking the dirty hay out of the stall.

"Oh," Ricky replied, "well, you are doing my job."

"There's four more stalls man, have at it!" He said with a grunt.

Monica and Emily had left at four in the morning so that they could drive to Crowley to get an early start at the Black Friday bargains. Jack wanted no part in fighting the crowds so he took off shortly after they left. He had planned on just driving around but ended up at the Lodge and decided to make good use of the pent up energy by cleaning the stalls. He knew the lodge was closed until Monday, but the horses sure didn't oblige, they could muck up a stall faster than he could clean it. Jack had been there for almost two hours when his friend Ricky showed up for his morning duties.

"Want a breakfast burrito?" Ricky asked from across the barn.

"Nah, stomachs in knots, I can't eat. That coffee sure smells good though." He answered.

Ricky hadn't planned on having company for breakfast so he was grateful he didn't have to share his food. He was only running on about four hours of sleep so he had a thermos full of coffee that he made strong enough to get up and walk on its own.

"Thanks." Jack said as he was handed the thermos lid full of steaming hot coffee. He hadn't realized how tired he was until that moment. He was hoping the strong brew would perk him up. He had a fitful night tossing and turning trying to wrap his head around Angela having his ring.

"You look like hell man. What gives?" Asked Ricky, as he bit into the breakfast burrito with extra jalepenos and habanero sauce.

"Just have a lot on my mind lately." He said.

"It's a woman, huh?" he asked matter-of-factly.

"Alright you got me." Jack said without elaborating.

Jack and Ricky had been friends for a long time. They both knew that if the other wanted to talk he would in his own way in his own time. They never pried into the others personal life.

Ricky just nodded in understanding and said, "Yep, a good woman will do that to a man."

Jack finished up his coffee as Ricky finished his meal and they both went about cleaning the stalls in silence.

— ~

"Welcome to the Dress Barn! Everything in the store is 30% off and everyone who comes through the door gets entered into a drawing to win a free makeover worth over $500." Angela announced over the loud speaker for what seemed like the umpteenth time today. Her throat was feeling scratchy and she was so tired she was afraid she would fall off the designer heels she wished she hadn't worn. Angela had been at the store since 4am making sure everything was in place for their black Friday sale. The sweet little ladies she usually saw in her store seemed to have turned into vultures at the mere mention of a sale. Angela wondered how they could give thanks on Thanksgiving and then the very next day feel no shame in staging a no holds barred race to see who could get the most bargains at the cheapest prices.

About mid-morning there was a bit of a lull in the fury of people hustling and bustling about in search of a bargain. Angela took advantage of this slump and decided to find a hiding place in the back. Dropping down into a comfortable chair beside the dressing rooms she gulped a half bottle of water, set the timer on her phone for fifteen minutes, and kicked off her heels before leaning back and closing her eyes for a quick cat nap. She was almost asleep and didn't notice when out of the dressing room beside her come Jacks sister Monica.

Monica saw Angela right away and tried her best to rush by her so that they could avoid the awkward meeting. She wasn't sure how her brother was going to handle things with her and she didn't want to be the one to make the first move.

In her haste to hurry by she lost her tight grip on the bags and dresses in her arms and right in Angela's lap landed a red patent leather purse she had bought for Emily.

"Sorry," was all she could say as she fumbled to pick up the purse and put it back in its bag.

"Monica?" Angela asked as she looked at her with weary eyes.

"Yeah, it's me. I was just doing a little shopping with Emily." She said as she gave up on trying to make her escape.

Looking around Angela asked, "Where is she?"

"Oh, she didn't want to try on dresses with me, she's next door at the candy store. I told her she could pick out one thing....probably has a whole basket full by now." Monica said

Angela just smiled. She wasn't sure what to say and she could see the nervousness Monica was trying to hide too.

"I didn't steal his ring." She blurted out. She figured she might as well get to it since it was hanging over both their heads.

"I didn't accuse you of that." Monica said cautiously.

"I know, but your brother sure did. He looked at me like he hated me, eyes all crazy and making accusations of working with his ex in some scheme to steal his daughter. I didn't even know the ring was still in my house. Dad was supposed to find the owner. I've had too much going on in my life to worry about a ring! I thought he knew me better than that. I know we only just met, but still, I didn't think he would think something like that of me. I don't even know his ex-fiancé. Why would I want to steal his ring?" By this time Angela was tearing up and trying to hide her face from Monica and any other customers who might be passing by.

Monica felt sorry for Angela. She knew how her brother's hot head got him in trouble and she didn't like anyone to have to be on the receiving end of one of his bad moods. She gave up trying to hold on to her purchases and dresses she had been trying on. Dropping the items in the floor and kneeing down she put her arms around Angela's shoulders and tried to comfort her.

"When do you get lunch break? Do you want to take an early lunch with me and Emily?" Monica asked before she really realized what she was doing. For some reason she liked this woman too, and wanted things to work out with her and her brother.

"I don't think Jack wants me anywhere near Emily." She sniffled as she hugged Monica. It felt nice to have Jacks sister so near. At least she wasn't accusing her of trying to take Emily or steal a ring.

Leaning back Monica winked at her. "What Jack doesn't know won't hurt him!"

Angela felt better after her lunch out with Monica and Emily. They had done a little more shopping while they waited for her to get off work. Her boss's son was filling in as the interim boss while he was on medical leave and he was very happy that she had come in so early to help out that morning that he was more than happy to let her leave at noon when things had finally settled down. Angela was glad for the early departure and was looking forward to her weekend off.

"I had fun with that angel today," said Emily on the drive home. "I hope daddy starts being nice to her again. I really like her."

"Me too honey, but let's not tell your daddy we invited her to our Thanksgiving Dinner." Monica said as she pulled out onto the main road to head home.

Walking up to the front door of Monica and Jacks parents' house Angela felt very out of place and worried that she had made a big mistake when she agreed to come to Thanksgiving Dinner as Monica's guest. Angela couldn't make her feet move as she stood there in the big yard holding the bowl of pasta salad she had prepared for the occasion. Monica told her not to bring anything other than herself and her appetite, but she felt ashamed to show up empty handed. Debating on whether to hightail it out of there before anyone saw her she realized she had missed her chance when she saw an older man pop his head out the front door. She had never met this man before but assumed it must be Jacks Father. He looked just like him except for the gray and thinning hair. He was as tall as Jacks 6'2" with shoulders just as broad.

"What have I got myself into?" She whispered to herself.

"Well, don't just stand there girl, get in here! We've been expecting you!" He called from the door as he motioned for her with his big muscular arms. Jack had told her he was a retired wrestling coach, and he still had the muscles to show for it.

Angela found herself relaxing as she sat and visited with Ashley and Max, Jack and Monica's parents. They were very nice down-to-earth people. Monica had called and told them all about Angela, or at least what she knew, and Angela found herself willingly volunteering any information they asked about her. Ashley said she knew Angela's Mother from her water aerobics class and told Angela that she had only heard good things about her. This made her smile. She was really beginning to like Jacks family; they all seemed so warm and friendly toward her, except for Jack of course.

— ~

"Ok Mon, now it's my turn, what did you do? Why did I just have to sit for three hours with that woman at our family Thanksgiving?" Jack hollered across the kitchen as he walked through the big wooden front door leading into his living room.

Monica had prepared most of the meal at her house that morning, and her mother insisted that she and Jack bring the leftovers home. Monica was keeping herself busy by stuffing what she could in Jack and Emily's refrigerator. Not knowing how to answer him she acted as if she hadn't heard him.

Knowing what she was doing Jack blocked her way as she was hauling another dish to the refrigerator. "You are not getting out of this one Mon. I expect some answers. You know how she hurt me and you still invited her to our Dinner? How could you?" He said with hurt in his eyes.

"Jack, I know how you feel, and I think you are wrong about her. She is good for you, and she is good for Emily. Didn't you see how her and Emily were bonding after dinner? They had a whole Barbie village set up in the living room. Now I ask you Jack, what other woman have you dated that would play Barbies with that sweet little girl of yours? She's telling the truth little brother; she was completely taken by surprise at you accusing her of having anything to do with Mystique. I even had Mom talk to her Mom; they are acquaintances from water aerobics. She confirmed the whole story about the ring. You have got to let yourself feel again Jack, or you are going to become a hermit. Is that what you want?"

Monica threw too many questions and thoughts at him at once. Jack didn't know what to do. His head was reeling from all that had gone down this past couple of weeks. He wanted to trust Angela. He wanted to trust his heart, but he was scared. Sighing loudly he turned and saw Angela's face on the TV screen.

9

"Anyone coming in contact with either of these two individuals should consider them armed and dangerous. Contact the authorities right away." Said the announcer loud and clear as Jack stared unto the eyes of the woman he just had dinner with and her ex-boyfriend Dewar Grant.

"Geez Mon, is that the woman you want getting involved with me and your niece? She's a fugitive!" he shouted over his shoulder.

Monica was busy cleaning the pots and pans she hadn't gotten to earlier in the day. Drying her hands on the dishtowel she slowly walked into the living room where Jack was still as a statue in front of the TV.

As she reached for the phone and started dialing Jack snapped out of his fog.

"What are you doing?" he asked in shock.

"What do you think I am doing? I am calling the police. We just spent hours with that dangerous woman." She said in confusion.

"Sorry, wrong number!" Jack said as he put the phone he had wrestled out of her hands to his ear and heard the 911 operator on the other end. Monica was confused as she watched her brother.

"What the hell Jack?" She asked.

"I'm calling her; she told me about Dewar, I want to warn her." He said as he punched her number into the phone.

Monica thought her brother had lost his mind. He was just ranting and raving about her possibly stealing a ring from him and now when they saw evidence of her sketchy behavior broadcast on TV he was calling her to warn her. She didn't understand him one bit at that moment.

"Ok, thank you." He said and hung up after only a couple seconds on the phone to Angela.

Jack sat hard on the couch a slumped his shoulders. Monica sat beside him and took him into her arms like she used to do when he was a little boy. With his head on her shoulder he said, "Her mom said she's been handcuffed and they are taking her to Baton Rouge. She has to fly to New York on the Red Eye so that she can stay in prison over the weekend and be there for trial early Monday morning."

Monica gasped. She couldn't believe the turnaround in her brother and she didn't know what to say so she just stroked the back of his head and kept silent.

"Monica, she told me about Dewar, she didn't help him, he must be up to something to drag her into all of this again so soon. She wasn't supposed to have to go to trial for this until January." Jack said between huge sighs.

Pushing him off her shoulder to get a better look at him she said, "What's going on Jack, just a few minutes ago you were furious at me for having invited her to dinner, and now you are wanting to defend her for an even bigger crime that you really know nothing of? What are you thinking?"

"Oh Mon, it just hit me. She's the one. I know it! Emily is right. I have never felt so sure of anything in my life. I was mad at you, and dad, and mom for going along with it, but when I saw her on TV all I wanted to do was protect her. Does that make sense? Am I just crazy?" He said as he looked at her for answers.

"No baby bro, you just sound like a man in love." Monica said.

"I think I am." He declared. "Do you think I can meet her at the airport before she goes?"

"Maybe, but I don't know if they will let you talk to her."

"Well, I've got to try, now don't I? She has to know how I feel." he said as he stood to gather himself and his jacket.

Turning around he asked, "You will stay here tonight and watch Em won't you?"

"Of course, you don't even have to ask. Now go find your gal!" she said.

With new purpose in his heart Jack raced to the airport. The highway was a blur of headlights. He didn't even worry about getting a ticket as he hit ninety in his big black truck.

— —

"What do you mean there's new evidence? The tired Lawyer shouted at the phone. Deep in sleep Amos did not appreciate being woke up.

"I don't know," said Angela, "You are my lawyer, you are supposed to know."

"Well, Dammit, I will meet you at the airport. Tell those boys in blue they better wait for me." he said as he sat up and dragged himself out of his comfortable bed.

Angela was in shock as she rode in the back of the police car to Baton Rouge. All she had been told was that there was a warrant out for her arrest due to new evidence in her case. She had no idea what this new evidence could be. She had told her Lawyer everything she knew and he assured her that he was going to get the charges dropped when she went before the judge in January.

It felt like hours as she sat in the back of the cramped little car like a caged animal. She couldn't bring herself to look out the windows for fear someone she knew would be passing by. Tears stung her eyes as she cried in silence.

"Jack, what are you doing here?" Asked Angela's Mother when he almost plowed her down in his sprint across the parking lot.

Although the run from his car was only a couple hundred feet Jack had to stop and catch his breath before he could talk to Gretchen. The weight of the unknown sitting on his chest made him feel as if he had ran all the way from home.

"I'm here to see Angela before she goes. I have to tell her I am sorry and I believe her about everything. I know this is all a big mistake. I don't know how I know since we barely know each other, but I do. We have really made a connection from our few times out together and our many conversations over the phone. I'm afraid I was uncouth tonight at Dinner and I feel bad. I just have to get things straight with her before she goes off to New York. I don't want to give her more to worry about. I think she has enough on her plate as it is." He said in a rush as he glanced around the airport for Angela.

"That's mighty big of you son." Said Ken as he put his arm around his wife's shoulders, "But I'm afraid she just got on the plane. They let us say a quick goodbye, but her lawyer said they just told him she wasn't going to be able to contact any of us until Monday after the trial."

"Oh no. I don't like this at all. What is going on?" Jack asked throwing his hands up in the air.

"We don't know, all they told us was there is new evidence that will prove her involvement with the theft of nearly two millions dollars over the past several years." Gretchen said in a monotone.

"You don't think she did it do you?" Asked Jack.

"We don't know what to think, this is all such a shock to us. Good night Jack, I am going to take her home now and try to catch some sleep." Said Ken with a half-hearted handshake.

Angela forgot about her fear of planes as she sat quietly trying to erase the feeling of being violated during the strip search that just occurred. The two officers had not been gentle as they ruffed up her body to make sure she was not carrying anything across state lines. Shuddering as she tried to forget the horrible feeling they gave her she didn't notice when she bumped the cup of coffee in her lawyer's hand.

"Whoa, watch out would you. I had to pull major strings to get them to leave the cuffs off while we were in the air. I am not too happy about having to get out of bed at this hour and fly half way across the country on the spur of the moment. You could at least let me drink this cup of hot mud they think passes for coffee in the airport lounge." He huffed at her.

Looking at him in disbelief Angela tried to bite her tongue and keep quiet, but she couldn't bring herself to it. "You think I wanted this? I don't even know what is going on. They didn't even let me keep my purse or my phone. I didn't get to bring any of my clothes with me. They took my shoestrings and even my belt. They strip-searched me and no one has even told me what this is all about. You are my Lawyer. I am paying you to keep my good name from being drug through the mud and you have the audacity to complain to me about coffee? I would kill for a cup of coffee right now! But do I get one? No! There is no telling what my parents think of me."

Tears ran down her face again and she wondered how much she could cry before she became dehydrated.

"Here." Was all he said as he handed her the cup of coffee.

"Thanks." she replied as she took a big swig of the liquid. Hot mud, as he had described it was quite fitting but somehow it hit the spot.

"They kept looking at my tattoo." She said after a few minutes of silence. "They even brought in a Chinese interpreter. Isn't that crazy?"

"Hmmmp." was his response to her as he tried to rub the sleep from his eyes to wake himself up.

"Evan, or Dewar talked me into getting it one night in Paris." She decided to go on to keep herself sane even if he wasn't really paying attention. "It's just a Chinese symbol for Peace. But I hate him so I'm getting it removed as soon as I can, just haven't had the time yet."

"Really? I have the same tattoo on my forearm." He said, surprising her with more than a grunt of response.

Pulling up his sleeve he showed her his tattoo. "See, same thing." He said.

"No, that doesn't look anything like mine." She said as she pulled up her own sleeve to show him the small tattoo on her shoulder.

"Strange," he said comparing the two. "Someone must have gotten it wrong then."

As they both pulled their sleeves down they sat in silence again as they waited for the two officers that had gotten up and were making their way toward them.

"Are you going to be good while we talk to your lawyer, or do we need to cuff you?" The larger officer said to Angela as they swaggered up to them.

Angela didn't respond other than shrugging her shoulders and just sipped her coffee as the tears kept coming.

"Let's go do this, where the hell do you think she's going to go, jump out the damn window!" Amos said as he jumped up and started walking toward the front of the plane where the other officers were gathered.

The two men eyed Angela suspiciously for a couple seconds before following Amos.

Angela sat there waiting for her Lawyer to come back with more information, for what seemed like an eternity. She had counted the seats on the plane and the windows more times than she could remember. Angela was afraid of what they might be saying. She had no idea what Dewar was capable of.

She did enjoy the fact that Amos got away with speaking so gruffly to the bunch of overgrown he-men that were holding her hostage on this plane. The plane that she was trying not to think about. Angela had always had a fear of flying and drove for days at a time to keep from having to fly when she would visit with her parents while in school.

Angela was almost in a panic over the plane ride when Amos made his way back to where she was sitting.

"Are you alright girl? You are sweating bullets." He commented as he sat beside her.

Amos just sat there grinning like the cat that caught the canary. Angela began to wonder if he had lost his mind. After a few minutes of the anticipation he said, "Aren't you going to ask me?"

"Ask you what?" She said wiping the sweat from her brow.

"What we talked about." He said but went on before she could say anything, "I think we may have found the key to get you out of this. Show me that tattoo again."

Now Angela knew he was crazy. Looking at him in confusion she pulled up her sleeve and showed him her exposed shoulder with the tattoo on it. All the while he had been messing with something on his phone.

"Yep, that's what I thought." He said.

Again he didn't wait for her reply as he thrust the phone in her hands with pictures of chines lettering.

"So what's all this mean?" She asked.

Not answering her question he asked one of his own. "You said Dewar talked you into getting that tattoo when you were in Paris?"

"Yeah, why." she asked.

"Had you been drinking?" He asked her.

"What's that have to do with anything. Yeah, we had been to dinner and were celebrating and I might have had a drink or two." She explained with confusion painted on her face.

"There it is." He said louder and with satisfaction in his voice.

Clapping his hands together like an excited child he kept repeating, "Hot damn, hot damn, hot damn!"

—- -◞

10

"How can I settle down Ken?" Gretchen asked as she was pacing the hardwood floor of their bedroom. She'd been at it since they'd returned home and he had tried repeatedly to calm her down.

The closer they got to their home the more the two of them realized they had been too hard on Angela. When the police had arrived on their doorstep shortly after nine they were taken by surprise. When the police told them that Angela may be a danger to them they became confused and frustrated and began to wonder just what she had been involved with when she lived in New York. They hadn't badgered her about moving back and she hadn't offered much in the way of explanation.

But they knew Angela was an honest person and they had never been wrong about trusting her implicitly.

Gretchen and Ken were both taken aback at the events of the evening. Neither had said much to Angela as she was whisked away. They had followed her to the airport and were allowed to talk to her for a few minutes before she had to leave, but neither of them knew what to say. On the drive home they both began to feel the full intensity of what was going on, and were beside themselves with worry for her welfare and her feelings toward them.

"We were awful to her Ken." Gretchen said.

"No we weren't dear, but we weren't good to her either." He decided to join his wife as she walked back and forth in front of their king-sized water bed. Finally she stopped pacing and smiled at him.

"Ok honey, you got me to stop, now let's figure out how we are going to make this right!" She said.

Hugging her he asked, "What do you think about a plane ride?"

— ⁓

"Daddy, you promise you'll be back by next weekend to go Christmas shopping, huh, huh, huh?" Emily said jumping up and down beside Jack as he was talking on the phone with his dad.

Monica, bless her heart, intervened and took Emily to the kitchen to help prepare supper while Jack finished his conversation.

After retiring from his coaching job at the university Jacks dad took on a part time management position with the Lodge. He loved showing tourists around the bayou. His main job was the business side of things, but he got out and manned the fishing and gator boats, and trail rides as often as he could. Jack knew that his father loved any extra time he could get at the Lodge so he knew he would fill in for him for a few days so he could follow his heart to New York.

"Sure son, I'll take over your duties this week, but just make sure you know what you are doing." He said

"I've never been so sure of anything in my life dad." He assured his father as he thanked him repeatedly for this opportunity and hung up the phone.

Jack had his big green army duffel that was usually reserved for the summer when he took youth on camp-outs in the bayou and taught them to live off the land, filled to the brim when his sister and Emily came in his room.

"When's the flight Jack?" Monica asked after watching him from the doorway for a moment in silence. She was proud of her baby brother.

"Seven in the morning, leaving out of Baton Rouge. I'll be gone before you two get up in the morning."

Walking over to inspect his bags Monica commented, "You sure will be a sight in New York with your army duffle! Can we say redneck?"

"I'm not going to impress those fancy-smancy New Yorkers, just Angela!" He said.

"Daddy, will you bring her back with you? We sure could use an Angel in the Christmas play." Emily Asked.

"I think we might just talk her into it baby!" Jack said smiling and picking Emily up in a big bear hug.

"Jack, let's not get ahead of ourselves, you have a lot of groveling to do before you talk that girl into anything." Monica said.

As he put Emily down she asked, "What is gravely-ing?"

"That's groveling honey and it's where your daddy tells your angel that he's sorry he's been mean and begs her forgiveness." Monica replied.

"Oh, ok, well daddy do real good groveling and bring my angel home." Emily said as she jumped up on Jacks bed and finished zipping his duffel bag for him.

"I sure will try sweetheart!" He said.

Jack didn't sleep at all that night. He was too worried he would miss his alarm so he laid there staring out the window at the black night that loomed on before him. Around 2 AM he gave up and hauled himself out of the bed to get ready for whatever awaited him in New York. He had no idea where she was going to be having her trial but figured that should be public information so he would just find a courthouse and hope for the best.

He wished he could pull out his old guitar and strum a few chords. He had taught himself to play at an early age and whenever he felt anxious about anything it always soothed him to put his feelings to music. When Emily was a baby and nothing seemed to calm her down, not a bottle, not changing her, not even rocking her, him playing a tune for her always seemed to do the trick. Jack smiled at the thought that he shared that commonality with his daughter. *I hope I'm doing right by you baby girl.* He thought to himself.

Jack flew down the highway heading toward the airport. There weren't many cars out that early in the morning and Jack had free reign of the highway. Monica was going to drive up with their Mother later in the day and pick up his truck. He didn't want to leave it all week at the airport but didn't want to put anyone out either. Lucky for him she had insisted on bringing it back home.

Once Jack was seated on the plane he began to get sleepy. He had made it to his first destination and had at least six hours to kill. With heavy eyelids he drifted off to dreamland.

— —

"Take my hand Ken, you walk too fast, I don't want to lose you!" Gretchen fretted as they boarded the plane early Monday morning. They had gotten ahold of Amos late Sunday afternoon and he gave them directions to find them in New York. They probably wouldn't make the trial that started at 1pm, but they would sure be there to greet their daughter when she got the verdict. Amos wasn't able to tell them many details over the phone but he assured them the outcome was going to be in Angela's favor.

"Honey, I am not going to leave you, quit your worrying. I'm right here." Ken whispered loudly as he stopped in front of Gretchen and she ran into the back of him causing the person behind her to run into her. This struck her funny as she imagined human dominoes tumbling down the aisle.

"Ahhhh," she gasped as they continued to be ushered to their seats.

"Is that Jack?" She asked as she squeezed her husband's hand. For a little woman she was very strong and he grimaced as he pulled his hand away shaking it and rubbing it with the other at the same time.

The stewardess seated them right behind the sleeping man so Gretchen was able to get a better view.

"It is him!" She exclaimed and then turned to tend to Ken who was still favoring his injured hand.

Jack awoke about an hour before the plane landed. He felt refreshed from the deep slumber he had been in. As he wiped his mouth for any drool that may have gotten away from him while he slept he felt a sharp tap on his shoulder. Angela's parents had been sitting right behind him all this time on the plane. Jack noticed her father roll his eyes as her mother gushed on about what a sweet thing Jack was doing for their daughter by surprising her in New York. Gretchen and Ken filled him in on where the trial was being held and the three of them shared a cab after the plane landed and they had retrieved their bags.

Angela had been relieved that she didn't have to spend the weekend in jail. When they arrived in New York early Sunday morning she had been taken immediately to a police station downtown where she had to endure a long lie detector test. Angela still hadn't been given much information about what was going on, but the officers must have been satisfied with her answers because she was put in the custody of her lawyer at a five-star hotel for the remainder of the weekend.

Angela's back was to them when Jack walked in with Gretchen and Ken. The three of them were nervous and didn't say anything as they quietly sat in the back row.

"All Rise, The court of....." The bailiff started rambling off. Angela didn't hear a word he said as she stood there nervously. When they were told they could be seated Amos had to grab her arm and make her sit. She was dressed in a designer black fitted suit that he had bought her that morning. She had on three inch heels and her hair and makeup looked impeccable. Outwardly she appeared to have it all together but inside she was a raging storm of emotions. She thought she might pass out from sheer fear. The only sign that she was nervous was the twitch in her right eye. She rubbed it furiously as Amos cleared his throat to get her attention.

"They called you to the stand." He said.

Standing slowly she wasn't sure how she was going to make it without falling flat on her face. Somehow she did it, though. After the swearing in, the female Judge, who reminded her of that woman judge on TV, turned to her rather than the opposing lawyer and shocked her as she said, "Little lady, we owe you a big apology."

The silence was audible as everyone in the courtroom waited for the judge to explain.

"We are very sorry that you have been dragged into this ugly matter. My only advice to you is to keep close guard on your good-natured innocence and mind the company you keep. You are dismissed from my courtroom. Your attorney will now take you in the back and explain things further." The judge said just before banging the gavel down hard.

The bailiff led a confused Angela back to the table where Amos was waiting with a smile. He too rose and followed them out of the courtroom.

Angela was surprised to see her mother, father, and Jack sitting in the very last row of seats with equally confused looks on their faces.

Angela saw Amos bend down beside her parents and tell them something as he was walking out.

When they got into the big cushy room in the back of the courthouse Angela was finally filled in on what was going on. She had never been to court before but was sure from what she had heard and seen on TV that this was unprecedented. Amos explained that it was her tattoo that saved her. What the two of them thought was just small talk on the plane actually changed the whole course of the proceedings. Apparently while they were in Paris "Celebrating" Dewar was actually setting up a foreign account to hide over two million dollars that he had stolen over the course of the years. The feds had been breathing down his neck and he knew he needed to lay low for a while so he decided to put his stolen money away until he felt it was safe. Dewar and Angela had been drinking but what he didn't tell her was that he had slipped something in her drink to make her forget the conversation he had with the tattoo artist. She was told later that she had picked out a Chinese symbol for peace and that was what was tattooed on her shoulder. The symbol was Chinese, but it read, "It's in the bag." That is why her tattoo didn't match Amos's.

The officers in the plane that first night had told him Dewar was going to be able to prove that she had been involved because she had where the money was hidden tattooed on her body. It took them a while to decipher the lettering and figure out what it meant, but they were able to ascertain that The Bauug, as it was actually called, was a French-Canadian bank where Dewar had an account that he had opened a couple weeks prior to their trip to Paris. He needed to go to Paris to sign some documents in person since it was such a large sum of money he had deposited. Amos had a feeling Angela wasn't involved after hearing her talk of the tattoo she despised. After they landed he was able to get her set up with a lie detector test to prove his theory.

Once that was confirmed to be legit they had to get a quickie court order so that Dewar and his Lawyer would have to agree to give him one as well. He was all set to take the lie detector test Monday morning when he lost his nerve and confessed to the whole thing. Amos told her it was only luck that he was able to contact Dewars parents through social networking and they had his Grandma call his lawyer. "I guess you're never too big and bad to get taken down by your 98lb 90 year old grandma! I guess it just goes to show you that misery loves company. I can't say that Dewars sentence would have been any less if you had been involved, but for some reason he felt the need to try and drag you down with him" Amos said in attempt at a lame explanation as he finished the story.

Tears welled up in her big brown eyes as she jumped up and hugged him. "Amos, I could just kiss you! I have been so worried; I didn't know what I was going to do if all this got pinned on me. I feel like I just won the lottery!"

"Well, I'm glad I could help you, really I am." He said as he turned his head to keep her from seeing the tears that were trying to force their way out of his own eyes. This weekend had been an emotional rollercoaster for him too. As much as he should be he really wasn't looking forward to going home. He knew his wife wasn't going to be there waiting for him.

"You just be sure to follow that Judges advice and watch who you trust. There are some pretty mean folks out there and they will take advantage of your generosity faster than you know it."

"Thanks again Amos." She said.

"Well, you sit tight for a couple minutes, I will let your parents and your friend know you are ready to talk to them. I have to be on my way to catch my flight home." He said as he hugged her once more and went for the door.

11

"What are you doing here?" Angela asked bluntly as Jack entered the judge's chambers behind her parents.

Before he could reply Gretchen spoke up and said, "Now, that's no way to greet someone who's flown across the country to be with you in your time of need, now is it?"

Angela just stared without speaking. She was confused by everything that had gone on the past week and Jack was just adding fuel to the fire.

"Amos has reserved us a couple rooms at the Hyatt and supper is on him tonight. He wanted to make sure we had comfortable accommodations after all this. Let's go eat and forget all about this craziness." Ken interjected to try and lighten the mood.

Amos had only secured two rooms for them since he was unaware of Jack's plans to fly up as well. The rooms were adjoining and the men took one and women the other. Once they were all settled in the four of them headed down to the hotel dining room for the elegant meal that awaited them.

When Angela's parents were engrossed in the menu and wine list she heard Jack whisper from across the table.

"I wanted to apologize for my behavior."

"I don't know what you mean, " she said coolly.

Gretchen and Ken were trying their best to stay behind the menu so that these two could hash it out. Jack had explained his being there and all he had put Angela through by giving her the cold shoulder at Thanksgiving the night just before she was arrested. He had begged her parent's forgiveness and now he was hoping to get the chance to explain to Angela.

"I want a chance to explain myself and beg your forgiveness. I think what we have could really go somewhere and I don't want to miss that opportunity because I am so bullheaded." He said.

"You don't have to worry about it. No big deal. I'm a grown woman, hell I've been arrested and accused of so many things lately that your accusations didn't phase me." She said while trying to keep her chin up and the tears at bay.

"Now Angela, I know you are hurting, and I know I have hurt you. What little time we have spent together has meant the world to me; I hope it did you too." Jack whispered louder this time.

"No, we're through." She said.

Jack was glad to see the waiter show up at the table right about then. He had laid it all on the line and she wasn't having a thing to do with him.

Lowering their menus she ignored the looks her mother and father were giving her. No one had said much about the current circumstances since she had seen them. Everyone was acting as though they were on some sort of vacation and it was frustrating her to no end. She knew she had to eventually forgive her parents for how they had made her feel, but she sure didn't have to play nice with Jack.

Angela was ready for a good night's sleep that evening. What little sleep she'd had in the last few days had been fitful. After showering and changing into one of the big fluffy terrycloth robes she'd found in the bathroom she was ready to call it a day at five past eight.

"Night Mom, she said as she walked past her mother who was watching a complimentary movie on the big flat-screen in their suite.

"Calling it a day early I see." Gretchen said with a sweet smile.

"Come sit here and talk to me first." She said patting the sofa beside her.

With hesitation Angela sat stiffly beside her mother.

"I'm sorry for how your Father and I acted when the police came. We feel so ashamed sweetheart, can you ever forgive us?" She asked with outstretched arms.

As much as she didn't want to Angela leaned into her mother's embrace and the tears came flooding down both their faces. Gretchen talked for what seemed an eternity, spilling her heart out to her daughter. She never wanted her to feel abandoned by her and Ken ever again.

Angela was happy and relieved to hear that her parents still held her in high regards. She had been terrified by the looks they had given her the night she was arrested, that they had lost their faith in her.

"Mom, I feel so pathetic. How could I get involved with someone like him?"

"You are a sweet girl and unfortunately there are a lot of people out there who will take advantage of that. You will know better next time." Gretchen said as she hugged her tighter.

"I hope so, Mom. I just want to go back home and forget all this." she said.

"I knew that you would honey, we have a plane booked for tomorrow afternoon. You can sleep in and we will leave after lunch.

"Thanks mom." She said.

Angela stayed on the couch with her mother and eventually fell asleep. Gretchen had covered her with a blanket and had gone back to watching her movie when Ken and Jack came through the door adjoining their rooms.

"Has the smoke cleared?" Ken asked as he leaned down and kissed his wife on top of her head.

"She's sleeping it off. She's had a hard time; I think she'll be ok though." Gretchen said.

Jack sat in the big recliner and took it all in. He felt like an intruder as he basked in the love these two clearly had for their daughter and each other.

"Poor Jack here has been through the ringer too I think." Ken mused.

"Well, son, you knew it wasn't going to be easy. You told us that on the plane." Gretchen said as she leaned over to pat his hand.

"I guess I shouldn't have come." Was all he said as he stood and went to the door leading to the balcony that connected both their rooms.

Angela awoke at three in the morning with her neck hurting from sleeping on the couch for so long. Rubbing it and rolling her shoulders to try and work out some of the kinks she looked around the hotel room. Her mother had told her that is what Amos whispered to them on his way out of the courtroom. He had paid for these two beautiful suites with his own money. In light of all that had gone on she was glad he had been her Lawyer. She would have to make a point to go to his office and thank him in person once she got back home.

Standing she decided to try and get a little more sleep. Even though, other than the pain in her neck she did feel very rested. She was thankful for the much needed sleep. She smiled when she remembered her mother had been holding her as she drifted off. It reminded her of when she was a child and would crawl in bed with her mom and dad whenever she was scared. Her mother always helped her to relax and forget her troubles.

As she made her way into the bedroom she found her Mother and Father wrapped in each other's arms in one of the big beds. Not wanting to disturb their rest she decided to go out onto the balcony to get a breath of fresh air.

She didn't notice at first that Jack was asleep in one of the lounge chairs. Angela walked up to the balcony overlooking the grand city. She realized she was glad she didn't live here anymore. Sidewalks and concrete weren't her style. She loved the small town she lived in and all the splendor Mother Nature had to offer. As she listened to the honking horns and far off shouts she missed the quiet peacefulness of crickets chirping and bullfrogs croaking. Closing her eyes to imagine herself back home already her thoughts were disturbed as a loud snore cut into them. Jumping back from the railing she now noticed a sleeping Jack lying flat in the lounger. With his bulging muscles almost breaking through his denim jeans, black t-shirt, and thick wiry blond hair sticking out from under his cowboy had he was using as a shield to any light that might try to deprive him of his sleep, she chuckled. He certainly didn't look like he belonged in the big city either.

— —

Jack had been having a hard time sleeping with Angela just a door away. He felt like a fool for chasing her to New York. Emily was his first and most important priority and he felt like he was not giving her a good example at the moment. After trying for a couple hours to sleep in the big quiet hotel room he had decided to go back out onto the balcony. Other than the noisiness of the city and the pigeons that kept landing on the balcony he found himself getting sleepy after sitting out there with his thoughts for a while. He had decided to try the big green lounge chair that looked inviting and was asleep in no time. He stayed that way until he heard some noises on the balcony that woke him. Jack was sure it was the birds again and was glad he had booked his plane ride back for tomorrow. "Damn birds!" He muttered.

"What was that?" he heard a voice ask from a few feet away.

Slowly he lifted his black Stetson and found himself looking into the sleepy-eyed face of an angel.

Seeing how her hair glowed in the moonlight Jack saw how his daughter could think she was an angel. If she would only kiss him with those soft supple lips of hers he would know for sure he was in heaven.

Chastising himself silently for those thoughts he sat up straddling the lounger with his long legs.

"Sorry, I thought I heard those obnoxious birds again!"

"What are you doing sleeping out here anyway?" Angela asked clutching her arms to her torso. She wasn't comfortable talking with him now and she was feeling the need to run back inside.

"Just couldn't relax in there I guess." He admitted. "What are you doing here? Last I knew you were out like a light on the couch."

"I was, and I must have slept hard without even moving. Now I have a crick in my neck that is killing me." She said rubbing her neck and wondering why she was relaxing a little more just talking to him.

"If you want I am an expert at back rubs. Just ask Emily!" He said patting the cushion next to him in hopes she would sit down.

Reluctantly Angela sat with her back toward Jack. As soon as he put his hands on her tight shoulders she felt the electricity tingle on her skin. She knew then that she should have went with her instincts and headed back inside when she had the chance.

"Nice night." Jack said trying to grasp at anything to get her talking.

"Yeah, a lot cooler than home. It must be near freezing out here. How were you sleeping there in just a t-shirt?" she asked as she pulled her robe tighter against her body.

Jack smiled at her back. He was so happy she was talking to him. "It's 52 degrees, rather warm for this part of the country this time of year. I guess I just don't get cold too easily. I am comfortable. Do you want to go in?" He asked.

"Not really." She confessed.

The two of them sat there talking for a long time after Jack finished rubbing her neck and shoulders. Both of them were surprised to see the sun coming up on the horizon.

"I can't believe we have been out here so long." Angela said.

"I'm sorry, you probably wanted to get some more sleep." he said.

Stifling a yawn she was just about to agree when a shrill noise started blaring throughout their hotel.

Without thinking Jack grabbed Angela's hand and they both ran back into the hotel suite where her parents were.

"That's a fire alarm Ang, get out and your mother and I will follow you!" Yelled her father over the deafening noise.

Angela grabbed her purse as she was pulled into the hallway by Jack. Not many people had made it to the hallway yet at such an early hour so they were able to get to the stairwell and race down the many flights of stairs to the bottom. Once they were safely outside they both stopped to catch their breath.

Angela then started laughing hysterically. Jack thought it a very odd reaction to have but he soon joined in. People stopped and stared at them as they rushed out of the building, but they didn't mind. The two of them strolled hand in hand to a bench across the street before they noticed they were still clinging to one another.

"What is so funny?" Jack asked as he continued to join in the laughter.

"I don't know, I jus, I, I, I jus....I can't talk." She finally blurted out.

She pulled her hand away from his and looked at him seriously and said, "Thank you, I needed that!"

"What are you talking about?" he asked.

"I needed a good laugh. I needed the exercise. And I needed a good friend to talk to. It just struck me as funny that I was worrying about all that's gone on the past few days and then a real catastrophe showed up, maybe, I hope not. I hope it was just a drill or a fluke, but in the light of all this it really made me see what my priorities should be." She said as she was looking at a confused Jack. "Do you understand?

"I think so." He said, "At least you called me your friend again. I think I can live with that!"

Jack and Angela rose as they spotted her parents coming out the side entrance of the hotel. Angela hugged Jack. He hugged her back but gave her a strange look. She didn't care. She was happy that they all made it out safely.

The four of them sat at an outdoor café about a half block away from the hotel for a couple of hours before it was determined to be a false alarm. The security cameras had gotten a clear shot of some reckless teens who had made it in a side door and pulled the fire alarm without being noticed by the hotel staff.

Although she knew she must be a frightful sight in her robe, mussed up hair, and bare feet, she was glad there was no real fire. She was happy to be let back in to get on some 'real' clothes. Although, with the early hour there had been many others who made it out with even less on.

Later in the day when she was standing in the long line at the airport waiting to be thoroughly interrogated once more before being allowed to board the plane she smiled. As much as she found it a hassle she was relieved that the airport was making everyone go through the same thing. This whole situation with Dewar had taught her, if nothing else, that she was never again going to trust someone solely on appearance. She was going to do her own thorough investigations from now on before trusting someone with blind faith. She probably wouldn't go as far as making them go through a metal detector or having them strip searched, but she smiled at the thought of that.

12

She found it hard to breathe when the two of them walked into the little shop. Clutching the Formica countertop it took everything she had not to turn and run. There was her daughter looking at a little brown teddy bear while her aunt wandered the shop. It had been months since she had seen Emily.

Mystique felt like a coward for the way she had snuck around just to get little glimpses of her daughter's life all these years. She knew she made the right decision when she left her with Jack, but she wished she could find some way to get to know her little girl.

When she found out she was pregnant with her she had called her mother. She was so excited and just knew her mother would be too. Her and Jack had made plans to get married. She thought all the pieces of her life were falling right into place.

Later that night her mother and father came to talk to her and congratulate her. They even brought the old beat up truck, that they drove only on special occasions, and took her to a fancy dinner across town. On the way back to the dorm she and her mother talked excitedly about her future. Mystique was happy she had such understanding parents who were supporting her through this. When they passed the college her mother's smile faded and she said, "Honey, we have to talk."

That was the beginning of the end of her happy life. Her mother and father told her they were not paying for any more of her schooling and did not approve of her marrying Jack. They were sending her to live with her cousin on his farm in Colorado. He was only a forth cousin so they told her she was to marry him and he would help her to raise the baby. Mystique was devastated. She was able to talk her parents into letting her get her belongings out of the dorm and tell her roommates goodbye. She couldn't face Jack. She loved him too much to break his heart and she couldn't bear to see the look in his eyes when he found out. All she could bring herself to do was leave a message on the marker board on their wall and hope he would find it.

Mystiques parents didn't let her have a chance to refuse to go with them. The only thing her father had said to her on the way to Colorado was "I'm not having a bastard for a grandchild young lady!" Her mother tried to explain to her that Jack would not give her the life she was used to, and they couldn't in good faith let their grandchild grow up "on the grid in corporate America." Mystique wished now that she had protested more. The life they had given her was based on free-thinking and acceptance to all, or so she thought. She sure didn't feel they were living up to those standards as she was whisked away to have her child hidden from his or her father. Mystique never thought her parents would act the way they were. As a child she was never allowed to have much social interaction with 'Mainstream Society' as they called it. They had lived in a nudist commune for most of her childhood. Not everyone had walked around nude, but they accepted everyone that lived there for who they were and what they chose to do with their life. She had chosen to go to college and was excited that her parents had allowed it. She thought they were finally giving her the freedom to make her own choices with her life to live it however she saw fit, even if it didn't fit into the pretty package they thought was acceptable. Now thinking back she realized it was only within the walls of the commune that they found it acceptable to empower their fellow neighbors to be themselves.

They drove for two days straight and when they arrived at her cousin's farm in the backwoods high in the hills in Colorado she was expected to marry Nicolas right away.

When they arrived and she got a look at the man her parents thought would be a better suitor for her than Jack she pled with all her might for them to take her back home with them. She made promises to move back home and to even stay away from Jack if they would just reconsider making her marry the frail old man who was standing there with the even older sketchy looking preacher. Her mother and father would not listen to any of her pleas. They kept telling her this was for her own good and the good of their grandchild. Nicolas was a bachelor and he had agreed to marry her and raise their child up to live off the land and learn the ways of their kinfolk. After a short wedding ceremony her parents drove off in the rickety old pickup and she was left standing there with her new husband.

Mystique was floored. She never thought her parents would treat her or their grandchild like this. She felt more like a prisoner than the loved daughter she always thought she was.

Nicolas McNay was a nice man....mostly...when he was sober, which was a rare occasion. He was a recluse who lived by himself and raised sheep and corn. There was no electricity or running water in his two-room shack. He slept in a hammock outdoors most of the time and let Mystique have the straw-filled mattress on the hard floor in the corner of the dirty abode she was to call home. Most nights she cried herself to sleep and kept herself busy during the day with cleaning, cooking, and caring for the animals. She rarely saw another person the whole time she was there. Occasionally someone would come to the door asking for the "medicine man" This confused her at first until she realized Nicolas was selling moonshine.

An old Indian woman started coming around near the end of her pregnancy and she delivered the baby for her right there on that same straw mattress. The birth was horrendous and long, she lost a lot of blood and didn't feel like lifting her head for the first two days afterwards. The old Indian woman sat with her and forced her to eat and move to get her strength built back up. Once she felt a little better she was excited to be a mother. Little Emily was the only thing she had to look forward to. Her parents hadn't tried to contact her, as far as she knew, since she had been there. Nicolas hadn't been much company. Besides having to pick up after him when he drank, he would barely speak to her or have much interaction with her at all. That first day was the only day he said more than two words to her, and that was only when the backwoods preacher made them exchange vows. Mystique had been frightened that he would try to kiss her or sleep with her, but he kept his distance and let her do her own thing.

After she had Emily her mood picked up a little. She was settling into motherhood and even found herself looking forward to the days ahead. She still had no contact with the outside world, but there at first she decided not to care. Emily was her world now. She decided that she would worry about the future when it came.

A few weeks after she had the baby Mystique had gotten her figure back. With the hard work on the farm, breastfeeding, and taking care of Emily it hadn't taken her long to slim down. It was then that Nicolas started paying more attention to her. Again, he was quiet as a mouse and a perfect gentleman when he was sober, but when he drank he started demanding his "husbandly rights."

It only happened a couple times at first and he didn't say anything about it the next morning so she figured it was his drunken state and it wouldn't amount to much. Then it stated happening every night and he would become more and more aggressive with his attempts. Nicolas started grabbing her around the waist and kissing her neck, pulling her hair and even tore her clothes once before he passed out in a drunken stupor. Mystique was becoming frightened for her safety but she figured she could defend herself as long as he kept away from Emily. He was, after all, at least sixty years old, probably pushing seventy she guessed. No one had ever told her how old he was, but he looked to be in poor health and walked with a cane.

Nicolas surprised her at breakfast one morning. He had picked a bouquet of wildflowers and had them sitting at the table when she started making the meal that morning. She was a little taken aback by this gesture but decided that he really was a good man when he was sober and had his head on straight. She decided that if this was going to be her life for the time being she would make the most of it and try harder to steer clear of him after supper. By that time in the day he was usually three sheets to the wind and stumbling around.

Whatever good intentions she had to try and make things more pleasant with this man were short lived when he came to the table that morning. He pointed to the flowers and then went straight for her and planted a big kiss full on her lips. Holding her wrists at her sides he said under his breath, "You'd better stop refusing me when I come to you at night. I was promised a wife and that is what I intend to get. And that little girl there is going to be mine too, she better grow up to be a good little hussy for her old daddy too!" With that he released her wrists took his big mug of milk and a couple biscuits and went out to the front porch to sit in his rocker.

Mystique was reeling from the shock of his boldness and the stale stench of his rot gut breath. Shaking, she cleaned the kitchen as quickly as she could and took her daughter into the little bedroom behind the only door in the small house. It didn't have a lock but the closed door at least offered some protection.

Mystique had never had him make advances at her while he was sober. She now knew that he was aware of the behavior, she had been hoping was just the alcohol. She also knew she could not stay there another night. When he threatened Emily she knew she had to leave. She shuddered at what he must have meant by saying Emily had better grow up to be a good little hussy for her daddy.

Mystique waited until she saw one of Nicolas's 'customers' show up to buy some moonshine. She then went to the coffee can she knew he kept his money in and stole a few hundred dollars. She was amazed to find it overflowing with large bills and hoped he wouldn't notice the few that were missing. She quickly packed a little satchel for herself and Emily so that they could leave when given the opportunity. She did not plan on staying the night there one more night. She was afraid that Nicolas was not going to take "no" for an answer the next time he approached her. She tried to go about her day like any other. She cooked the noon meal of salted venison and vegetables from the little garden she had been keeping out back. She was thankful that she still had a few Benadryl left amongst her meager belongings and crushed a few of them up and seasoned them in Nicolas's food making sure not to get any in hers. She hoped he wouldn't notice the distinct taste. If she was going to leave she had to do it now or never. She couldn't count on the Moonshine to put him under.

A couple hours after lunch Nicolas was snoring in the rocking chair on the front porch. Mystique took the opportunity to gather her daughter in her arms and make a break for it. She slipped by Nicolas as he snored loudly and then mumbled something in his sleep. She didn't wait to see if he was waking up as she started running and didn't stop until she was deep in the woods. With only a few hours left of daylight she knew she had to find shelter before the night set in.

She ran when she could and walked fast the rest of the time. Night was falling on them and she was weary beyond belief and worried that she would have to try to sleep in the deep woods with her young daughter. Mystique was just about ready to find a place under the trees to use as a shelter for the night when she stumbled upon a shack in the woods. At first she was scared that she had been walking in circles and came right back upon Nicolas's place. Tears of frustration were streaming down her face and her daughter was drenched and wailing, when a cold hand clamped down on her shoulder.

From that point on her luck changed for the better. The hand that scared the wits out of her had belonged to the old Indian woman who had delivered Emily. Mystique was worried at first that she would take her back to Nicolas. She rambled her story through sobs and ragged breathing while the old woman stared blankly at her. Then the woman took them both in the house, fed Mystique, changed and fed Emily and ushered them out to her rickety old wagon with a mule hitched to it. At that point she didn't know yet whether the woman was taking her back to

Nicolas or what. She kept asking the woman, who only nodded her head from time to time and directed the mule down a narrow path.

They rode along in the mule-led wagon for about an hour and a half before they came upon a Bed and Breakfast tucked away in the foothills of the vast landscape. No other sight had ever been as beautiful as that little Bed and Breakfast. The old woman stopped abruptly right at the front door. She hopped off the wagon and hobbled her way over to the entrance. She spoke swiftly to the elderly man who answered the door suspiciously and then came back to the wagon where Mystique was waiting anxiously with her sleeping daughter held close to her body.

When the woman got back to the wagon she muttered something that Mystique didn't understand and motioned for her to get off the seat. Once she was standing, with her small bag slung across her shoulder, and her daughter still held tightly in her arms, the old woman took her face between both her hands and kissed her firmly on the lips. and then said, "be a good girl!" With that she turned and rounded the wagon and stepped up to ready herself for her journey back home.

Mystique never even knew the woman's name but she had given her the gift of freedom and for that she was grateful beyond words. When she ambled into the foyer of the quaint little Bed and Breakfast the gentleman behind the counter quickly pulled out a key and showed her to a wonderful little room with patchwork quilts and doilies thrown everywhere.

She barely noticed the room full of trinkets and dust collectors. She had her sights focused on the phone on the nightstand. Holding the receiver for a few minutes she hesitated before calling the only person she could think of, other than Jack, who would care as much about her daughter's well-being as she did.

"Yes, I'll accept the charges." Said Monica hesitantly. She was confused that her Brothers ex-girlfriend would be calling her at all, and at such a late hour she was more than a little concerned.

14

"A unt Mon, Aunt Mon, look at this cute little bear, can I get him?" Emily asked as Monica came up behind her.

Monica hated keeping things from her brother, especially about his daughter. She knew he would be furious with her, and wouldn't understand why she brought Emily to Mystiques antique shop.

Monica had known about Emily weeks before Jack did. Mystique and she had stayed with Monica in her little apartment before she got up the nerve to approach him about his daughter. Of course, Monica hadn't told Jack that she had helped his ex to get back to Louisiana or everything else that had happened since that fateful day. She always meant to tell him, but now it had been six years and she still didn't know how or what to tell him. Emily didn't know that Mystique was her biological Mother, but the guilt was killing Monica. She knew that both Emily and her Mother deserved more than passing glances at one another.

"Aunt Monica!" Emily shouted, disrupting her thoughts.

"Not now honey, it's too close to Christmas. Let's see what Santa brings you. Today we're just looking for presents for Grandma, Grandpa, and Daddy." She said.

"And the Angel, let's get her something too!" She said as her eyes lit up.

"Ok, we'll find her something pretty. That's a good idea honey." She said as she took Emily hand in hers and directed her toward the counter where Mystique was waiting for them.

Monica made her purchases and small talk with Mystique. Neither of them wanted Emily to be suspicious of why they really drove all the way to Lafayette to look at antiques. There were, after all, hundreds of little shops just like this all across the state.

"That's a pretty little girl you have there." Said Mystique hoarsely, barely above a whisper.

"Thank you." Monica said, playing along and patting Emily on the head.

"This is my Aunt Monica," she said, "My daddy is her brother, we don't know where my mommy is, but Daddy says she loves me. I know an angel though, and maybe she'll be my new mommy." She continued, excited to have an adult to pay attention to her.

"I'm sure your Mommy loves you more than you will ever know." Said Mystique as she handed the receipt to Monica and grabbed for a tissue to hide the tears that were threatening to fall.

Monica ushered her out the door as she offered a quick smile to Mystique.

"Thank you!" She saw Mystique mouth to her just before she turned to go into a stock room.

That had been the first time Mystique had talked directly to Emily and Monica was worried that she would ask questions about the teary-eyed sales lady. She hadn't even noticed she'd been holding her breath until she exhaled loudly when they were a few paces from the antique store.

"Where are we going next?" Monica asked her niece.

"Let's get candy!" She said as she started jumping up and down.

"Whoa, do you think you need any more candy little one?" She asked

"Yeah, yeah, yeah!" She said pulling Monica by the arm toward the candy shop they had become very familiar with over the years.

Jack made it home early Tuesday morning. He hadn't had much sleep on the plane so most of the day Tuesday was spent snoozing. He and Angela did find time to talk to each other on the phone Tuesday evening and had made plans to go on a real date Wednesday. His felt like he had been on an emotional roller coaster this past week that had finally came to a halt. He was thankful for the much needed rest and the peace of mind he now had. However, he felt like he could get another forty-winks in at any moment.

Emily and Monica came busting in the door late Tuesday night with their arms loaded with shopping bags.

Monica sorted the bags and left Emily's in her bedroom. She would be by the next evening after church to help her wrap the presents she had bought for her daddy and grandparents. Monica stood for a moment looking around the room where her niece had grown up. A framed picture of the three of them at church camp from the past summer made her smile. She was proud of her brother for the wonderful job he had done with Emily. The little brown hamster innocently chewing on a small piece of wood atop Emily's nightstand stopped to stare as she sat on the bed to get a better look at the pictures and treasures her little niece held so dear. Emily kept everything neat and organized. She was a sweet little girl who was loved by all the people she knew who were watching over her from these memories frozen in time. Monica sighed as she stood. She wished she could give her the picture and address Mystique had slipped into her hand as they had walked to their car earlier in the day. Emily hadn't noticed the brave gesture. She was too busy recalling what she had purchased for her daddy out of her allowance she had been saving. She was so excited. This was the first year she had bought anything for anyone with her own money. Monica was sad that she was growing up so fast. She was also scared to death of the task she knew she had to do. She promised Mystique and her parents many years ago that she would tell Jack and Emily what really happened that awful summer. She knew she had to do it now; she just had no idea how.

She couldn't bear looking into those sad pleading eyes of Mystiques. She knew she had been waiting for Monica to introduce Emily to her just like they had planned all those years ago.

Monica felt like she had an elephant sitting on her chest that wouldn't budge and wouldn't be ignored any longer. Emily, Jack, and Mystique all deserved the truth. *The truth is supposed to make everything better right?....but maybe not this time.....* She thought to herself as she made her way to the front door.

She barely paid attention as she hugged her brother and kissed her niece, before making her retreat.

As she drove home Monica replayed the encounter with Mystique over and over in her head. She needed some answers and they weren't coming easily. Instead of turning down the lane that led home she stayed on the highway and drove until she saw Ricky's sign lit up in the distance.

"You look like you could use some company." The stranger said as he pulled up the barstool next to Monica

"Can I buy you a drink?" He asked

Holding up her martini glass she smiled again.

"Ok, I guess that is just a cheesy line every guy thinks he is supposed to say when he sits next to a pretty girl at a bar. My name is Amos Andrews, by the way." He said extending his hand. Monica noticed the tan line on his ring finger right away.

Well, damn. Amos thought to himself when he saw the thoughts going through her mind. They jumped off her face as if she had screamed at him to take his cheating ass straight to hell.

"Wait!" He said a little too abruptly as she was standing to walk away.

Against her better judgement Monica stopped to hear what he would say next, but before he could get a word out Angela and another girl walked up and started talking to Monica.

"What are you doing here?" Monica asked Angela.

"Just hanging out with my friend for a little bit tonight." She replied.

Monica looked at the girl who had just walked in with Angela. She looked like she was half in the bag already.

As her friend walked away Angela leaned over to whisper to Monica, "That's Denver, her husband owns this bar, you remember her don't you? She was in grade school with me when you were a teacher's aide."

Monica nodded as she watched Denver stumble into the back of the bar and lean up against a man she knew wasn't Ricky.

"She and Ricky are on the outs, she's just trying to make him jealous, but all she's doing is giving him more reason to leave her. In all reality, I think that is her plan." Angela said shaking her head as she watched her friend make a fool of herself. All the guys in the bar know she's Ricky's wife and know to stay as far away from her as they possibly can. Ricky is no slouch and he wouldn't hesitate to make mulch of anyone who rubbed him the wrong way.

"Hmmmp, must be going around!" They heard Amos say from his seat at the bar. He had not been trying to eavesdrop, but they were standing very close to him and he couldn't help but hear.

"What's that?" Monica said, annoyed that this stranger was still sitting there and was now listening in on a conversation that he had no business with.

"Amos!" Cried Angela, "What are you doing here?"

Before he could answer Monica interrupted by saying, "You know this lying, cheating, bastard? He was trying to hit on me and I can clearly see where his wedding ring belongs!"

Looking from Monica and then to Amos's ring finger where she was pointing Angela said, "Oh, I guess things didn't work out with your wife after all. I'm sorry."

"Me too." He said as he gulped down the last of his long-neck and motioned for the bartender to bring him another.

It was then that Monica really looked at him. She knew the name Amos from Angela talking about her attorney. This was most certainly him. He wore his Armani suit quite well and the five o'clock shadow bristling his face gave him a rugged look. The muscles rippling beneath his gray suit looked like they belonged to a lumberjack and not a man who worked nine to five.

Angela quickly thanked Amos for the room and accommodations he had set up for her and her parents in New York. They spent a few minutes making small talk about the fire alarm at the hotel, and he gave her a brief update on her ex and how he was going to spend the next twenty years behind bars. She hugged his neck and kissed him on the cheek as she jumped up to rush to Denvers aide as she saw her sit on the floor beside the juke box.

"See you at church tomorrow night!" She called over her shoulder to Monica.

"Really?" She replied.

"Yeah, Emily talked me into being the Angel for the Christmas pageant." She hurriedly said.

Smiling to herself Monica sat back down at the bar next to Amos.

She knew it wasn't a good idea to drink her troubles away but at this point she didn't care. Angela being here made her feel worse. She was such a lovely girl and so good for her brother. Monica was scared to death to make waves by telling Jack that she has kept in touch with Mystique all these years.

She sighed as she threw back the rest of her drink and did as Amos did to let the bartender know she was in need of another.

He gave her a sideways glance and smiling he said, "I tried to tell you I wasn't the jackass you thought I was at first."

"Hi Amos, My names Monica." She said, ignoring his remark and making her introduction.

15

*J*ack was excited for his daughter and Sister to get back from church. Practice for the Christmas play was taking too long and he was pacing the floor with anticipation for his late night date with Angela. He almost bombarded them as he jumped up and grabbed his jacket when they made their way to the front door.

"So where are you taking me?" Angela asked with a sly grin when she slid into Jacks pickup truck.

"Anywhere you want to go, my lady." He said matching her seductive tone.

Laughing she kissed him on the cheek and stayed sitting right up next to him in the middle of the cab. It felt nice to have her warm thigh pressed up against his.

"What was that for?" He asked innocently as he touched his face where her lips had just been.

"Just for believing in me and being there for me. It means a lot to me." She said before adding, "You mean a lot to me too. I think I like where this is going."

She couldn't believe she was being so forward, but the words were out there and she had meant them.

"I feel the same way." He said as he pulled the truck out of her driveway.

"Do you trust me?" he asked with raised eyebrows.

"Of course I do." She said. Even though it had been less than a month since she met this man, she felt like she had known him forever.

"Good, I know the perfect spot." He said and kept driving with one hand and entwined his fingers with hers with the other.

Jack took Angela to the Lodge where he worked. It was late and no one was around except for the two of them. Hand in hand they strolled the grounds. Other than her few years in New York, she had grown up in this area so she was well aware of the Lodge and all the excitement that could be found here. She had come here as a teenager with the youth group to go zip-lining. A couple years later she got to ride a donkey on a slow trail ride. Jack told her about all the other tourist attractions and how he would try to scare the city folk with his tales of big gators when he took them on the boat down the bayou. If she were to be completely honest, the stories about the gators were starting to frighten her a little bit. Jack noticed this when she grabbed his arm a little tighter. That just made him smile. He knew where he was going and wouldn't let anything harm the woman he was quickly becoming so fond of.

Jack stopped on a hill overlooking the small town. It was a beautiful clear night. The stars were shining down on them and the night air was only slightly cool as a breeze teased the skin on their bare arms.

"Arm you cold?" He asked as he turned to face her while pushing a stray lock of hair away from her face.

"No, I'm good." She replied.

"Thank you for being so good with my daughter. She was pleased that you agreed to be the angel in the play." He said

"She's a precious girl. I like spending time with her." She said.

Jack leaned down and took her by surprise and kissed her passionately just as the words finished passing from her lips.

It didn't take long for the surprise to fade and emotion to engulf them both.

Jack slowly raised his arms to her waist and drew her closer as their kiss deepened. On her tiptoes Angela found herself pulling him closer as their mouths parted and lounges touched. With her hands in his hair Angela moaned causing his pulse to race even faster. Taking a chance he raised one hand even higher as he cupped her soft breast. He was fearful that he was going too fast and didn't want to rush her, when she calmed his fears by pulling one hand away from his tussled hair and finding the buttons on his shirt. She undid a few and ran her hand along his bare chest. With all the strength left in him he pulled his lips from hers and looked deep into her eyes and said, "I think I am falling in love with you. I don't want this to be just a fling; I don't want us to take things too fast."

Panting ever so softly she said, "Jack, I feel the same way." And hugged him close laying her head against his still bare chest where her fingers had just been toying with the thick hair that was peeking out.

"Can I ask you something?" He said as she felt him tense up.

Stepping back slightly she dropped her hands to his and held them.

"Will you marry me?" He whispered as he leaned over to her ear and then dropped a kiss on her neck.

Angela was sure she had not heard him right. He had just told her he wanted to take things slow and not rush into anything. She couldn't possibly have heard what she just thought she did.

Straitening up after a couple minutes of silence he had a somber look on his face.

"Jack, what's wrong?" Angela asked.

"Didn't you hear me?" He asked is reply.

"I'm not sure I heard you right?" She said.

"Angela, I am in love with you. I think I have felt this way since the first time I saw you. I know it's soon, and I really don't want to scare you, I just have all these feelings bottled up and I have to get them out. I know I want to spend the rest of my life with you. When we are apart I find myself daydreaming about the next time I'll see you. I know I'd never be complete if you weren't a part of my life. We don't have to get married right away, but with you I don't want to take things too far without making a commitment to you. Do you understand? I hope I'm not making a complete fool of myself." he said it all in a rush to make sure he got it all out before clamming up.

"Oh, Jack, I am in love with you too. I know it's soon, but I agree, I feel like I have known you forever. Yes." She said and hugged him tight.

"Yes, did you say yes?" He screeched.

As she began giggling and nodding her head he picked her up and started spinning her around.

When he stopped he put her down and took her hands in his and kissed each one tenderly.

"Angela Baker, you have made me the happiest man alive! I promise to do right by you and always treasure you and our life together. Thank you."

With that he leaned down and kissed her softly on her forehead. Then he moved down to her waiting lips and kissed her deeper and swept her up into his arms and started carrying her down the hill.

Jack and Angela spent the night in a cottage that was once used by business men who took retreats at the Lodge. It hadn't been used in years, but Jack liked to stay in it from time to time when he needed to get away. Tonight he felt it was the perfect place to take Angela and get away. Jack built a fire in the stone fireplace, and they ate sandwich crackers and snack cakes Jack kept stashed in the cupboard, for supper. Surprisingly, although nowhere near five-star, It was the most romantic meal Angela had ever shared with a man. After their meager meal they snuggled up on the floor in front of the fireplace. Both Jack and Angela knew the other was not innocent when it came to the opposite sex but they found themselves feeling shy when they realized they were going to join together not only physically but spiritually and emotionally as well.

The next morning Angela awoke early. The fire had died down and sunlight was streaming through the plate-glass window.

"Morning beautiful." Jack said as she turned to look at him.

"Did I wake you?" she asked.

"Nah, just been staring at the woman I'm going to spend the rest of my life with and wondering how I got so lucky." He said.

Angela smiled at him and pulled him down closer to her.

They spent the morning wrapped in each other's arms making love and making plans for the future.

When Jack dropped Angela off at her house early that afternoon he didn't want to let her go.

"I had a great time." He said.

"So did I." She said as she leaned in for another kiss.

"Are you sure this is what you want?" he asked again.

"More than anything. This is where I am meant to be." She said pointing to his heart and kissing him again.

"I will call you later. I love you." She said as she opened the door to her parents' house.

On his way home Jack wasn't paying attention to the car that was tailing him.

16

Jack didn't know who owned the red Desota that stopped down the street from him, and he couldn't place the figure that was sitting behind the wheel. The stranger parked on the curb a few car lengths away but kept the engine running. He knew all the neighbors vehicles and those that were normally seen in the neighborhood. The hair on the back of his neck rose and cold chill come over him before he chided himself to knock it off. He decided that this must be a friend or relative of one of his neighbors and that was why he didn't recognize the car. At that thought he quickly forgot about the foreign car and grabbed his jacket after he put his truck in park. Jumping out he had a spring in his step thinking about the promises and plans he and Angela had made. He couldn't wait to tell his sister, and he knew Emily would be ecstatic over her Angel.

"Jack!" Shouted the stranger who still sat in the car as he was turning the doorknob he had just unlocked.

"What the heck? Who is that?" He muttered to himself.

Although the stranger was unbeknownst to him with the dark shades and ball cap sitting low he recognized the voice. Jack hadn't heard that voice in almost seven years. Stopping in his tracks his blood ran cold.

"Jack?" The voice called again, this time with more of a questioning tone.

Slowly he made his way to the little car whose driver was removing her glasses and cap. Holding her hand out the window she waved. "Jack it's me, Mystique"

Walking up to the car he crossed his arms as he said, "I know who you are, what I don't know is what makes you think you have any right to show your face around here. How in the hell did you find me?"

Pulling her arm back inside the car she looked away from him and stared down the street as she said, "I think it's time we talked, Jack."

"What makes you think I have anything to say to you? I sure don't want to hear anything you have to say to me." He shouted at her.

Mystique exhaled loudly and reached over to the passenger's seat and picked up the brown teddy bear that Emily was eyeing while at her store. She didn't know if Jack would accept it or not, but she turned to him and held it out the window. "Please give this to Emily, She was looking at it a couple days ago and I want her to have something from her mom for Christmas."

Jack felt his breath catch and his chest tighten. Emily had been shopping with Monica a couple days ago and they had not said anything about running into Mystique. Surely she was mistaken.

"What are you talking about?" He asked not making a move to take the brown bear with the red ribbon tied around its neck.

Mystique was confused, she knew Monica said she and Jack would have to wait until the right time to tell Emily about her, but Monica had assured her that she would tell him about the unusual circumstances of her disappearing.

"Well?" He interrupted her thoughts.

Putting the car in gear she pulled the bear back inside and choked out, "Tell Monica to call me!"

With that she drove away. Jack couldn't believe that had just happened. He hadn't had much sleep the night before while he and Angela were at the Lodge, so he almost thought he had been hallucinating and had imagined the whole thing.

Jack was still fuming when Emily got off the bus a couple hours after his encounter with Mystique. He had forgotten that she was bringing a friend home to play, so his plans to talk with her about her and Monica's shopping trip went by the wayside.

He tried to feel her out with as much tact as he could but he didn't get anywhere. Emily had just told him about all the pretty things she and Monica had seen and where they had eaten. She didn't seem to be hiding anything about seeing Mystique, so he hoped she didn't know.

Jack knew Emily deserved to know about her Mother, but all he knew was that she left that little girl with him when she was barely out of the womb and she hadn't tried to contact him since. What could he tell her about her mother? He had told her how pretty her Mother was and that he was sure she would be proud of her. Emily had never really asked much about her Mom, and for that he was grateful. When Angela had come into his life he found out that Emily had prayed for a Mommy, so he knew there was hurt there, whether she was mentioning it or not.

Jack had calmed down considerably over the course of the afternoon. He found himself enjoying playing dress up with his daughter and her friend Becca. After that the three of them had made root beer floats. They were all lounged in the living room singing Christmas carols while Jack played his guitar, when Monica stopped by after work.

Jacks expression immediately changed and he stopped playing when he saw his sister standing there listening to them.

"I think that's enough music for tonight girls. You better go get cleaned up and I'll take you out for pizza before we take Becca home." He said.

The two little girls didn't notice the change in Jacks mood. Too excited about the special treat in the middle of the week on a school night, they bounced their way out of the living room and headed down the narrow hall toward the bathroom.

Monica didn't notice the chill in the air or the daggers he was shooting at her as she walked by him and into the kitchen.

"I brought some brownies we had left over at the bakery. I know they're your favorite." She said.

Jack just stared at his sister. The words Mystique had spoken echoed in his mind. He couldn't imagine Monica keeping in touch with her all these years. As far as Jack knew they had only met each other one time back when he was in college at one of his wrestling meets.

"Monica, are you going to stick around? I need to talk to you about something after I take the girls for pizza. Or you can come with us if you want." He said coldly.

"I ate a late lunch today," she said and then hesitated before adding," But I can go with you if you need to talk."

"No, just be home, I'll call you later. What I have to say isn't for Emily's ears." He said.

Monica left when Jack and the girls left. After giving Emily a big bear hug she reached for her brother to do the same, as she always did, but he barely slowed down to acknowledge her before jumping in the cab of the truck and slamming the door in her face.

Monica was confused by her brother's behavior. Emily had stayed at her house the night before since Jack and Angela had a late date. She assumed his odd behavior had something to do with Angela. Since he said it was not for Emily's ears, she hoped it was not bad news. Emily was so excited that her daddy was officially dating her "angel." She knew the little girl would be devastated if things had gone sour with them already.

When Monica got home she found it impossible to concentrate on anything. With Jacks impending news and the situation with Mystique on her mind she couldn't sit still.

The handsome lawyer she had met at the bar earlier in the week had been a good sounding board for her. After she found out he was not the creep she had first thought him to be, she found herself chatting with him for a good portion of the evening. He told her about his failed marriage and she told him about the situation with Mystique. Monica figured since he was a lawyer he was someone she could be honest with. It had been nice to have him to talk to. Although they both admitted they didn't know what they would do if in the others shoes, he did offer some good advice when he told her to come clean and face the truth. "That's the only way you'll ever find peace with the situation." He had said. She realized that was what she had to do, but how and when were causing her great frustration.

She decided to forget about that for now and try to spruce up her house for Christmas. She had what seemed like hundreds of boxes of decorations her grandmother had kept throughout the years, up in the attic. Hauling them down gave her a little exercise and took her mind off her worries.

She was un-wrapping a delicate glass figurine that had been carefully tucked away the Christmas before, and remembering the year her grandmother had purchased it when she was just a little girl about Emily's age, when the phone rang. Deep in thought Monica jumped and had to fumble to keep the priceless heirloom from crashing at her feet.

With a catch in her voice she answered the phone on the third ring.

"Monica, it's me." Jack said.

"What is going on little brother? You have had me in a tizzy all night with worry." She said.

"I don't know, maybe you can tell me. Is there something you need to tell me Mon?" He asked through gritted teeth, with more than a little anger in his voice.

Monica was stunned into silence at his tone. He couldn't know about Mystique, she thought, so she assumed he must be upset over something else.

When she recovered from her shock she asked, "Did something happen with Angela on your date last night?"

"Nope, Angela and I are fine. That's not what this is about. Someone stopped by here earlier. Do you know who that might have been?" He asked. She could hear that he was seething with anger.

"I think I might, but you have to believe me, this is not how I wanted you to find out." She said. Monica was almost hyperventilating by this time. She didn't think that Mystique would have the nerve to go to Jacks home.

"Jack I'll be right over." She choked out as she hung up the phone.

"Dammit!" He said into the dead receiver. He had hoped he was wrong about this.

As soon as he hung up the phone he went out onto the porch to wait for Monica. It would only take a few minutes to drive to his house and he wanted his angry face to be the first thing she saw when she pulled in.

Jack was all ready to pounce when Monica put the car in park and got out, but then he saw the tears running down her face and saw her hand wrapped up in a towel. She was holding it against her chest as she made her way across his lawn.

"My God Monica, you are a mess! What did you do?" he asked with more concern than anger in his words now.

"I, I, I, cut my, my, ha ha hand on on the Ch Ch Christmas ornaments." She stuttered through sobs.

"Well my goodness, get in this house. You are dripping blood all over the porch. How bad is it?"

Monica had been dreading this moment so much that in her rush to get out the door she stumbled on a box of Christmas bulbs and landed her hand right on top of a big glass ball as she fell in the floor. Adrenaline must have kicked in at that point because she was able to pull out three large shards of glass without winching before she wrapped her hand in a dish towel and headed out the door. Now that she was standing here she could feel that throbbing take over. Her tears of frustration were now mixed with tears of pain.

Jack had her sit on a stool at the kitchen sink as he slowly un-wrapped the blood soaked dish towel. It didn't take long for him to see that the wounds were deep and she needed to have it examined at the emergency room.

"I'm calling Angela!" He said as he wrapped her hand back in a clean tight bandage.

"I know she'll watch Emily and I am taking you to the ER, no argument!" He said.

She just nodded.

On the way to the ER she said, "oh Jack, it's so terrible, much worse that you could imagine. I guess I just hoped she would forget about it and we could all move on."

"Mon, that doesn't even make sense, you don't forget about having a baby. Stop talking you are apparently losing too much blood, you must be in shock!" He growled as he pressed down on the accelerator.

The emergency room was, for the most part, empty that night so Monica got right in without having to wait. After they cleansed her wounds and made sure there was no more glass in her hand she was stitched up and released by ten.

Jack had been by her side the whole time but neither of them had said anything more about the reason she had rushed to his house in the first place.

"That was nice of Angela to stay with Emily tonight." She said, trying to find some common ground.

"Yep." Was all he offered in response.

When they were back in the parking lot Jack turned on her. "I am still so mad at you. I could spit nails Monica!" He said as he paced in front of his truck with balled fists. "Tell me everything."

The pain meds she had been given were making her a little drowsy so she went to the passenger's side and got in. Monica figured if Jack wanted to hear her story he would follow.

He did. After he hit the hood with his fist.

Cussing under his breath he slid in the cab but left the door open. He wasn't sure he wanted to hear what she had to say so he wanted the door open. For some reason he knew he didn't want to be closed in with the awful truth that was coming

"Well?" He asked.

Monica started slow, telling him about the night she got the call from a frantic Mystique asking her to pick her up at the Inn in Colorado. She then went on to tell him the harrowing tale she had been told when she got there.

"I brought her and the baby home to my little apartment. She made me promise not to tell." Monica said quietly and looked at Jack for a response. When she got none she went on.

"Her behaviors were so odd. She was a good mother, for the most part; sometimes she would forget to change Emily. Or she would try to give her a bottle after she had just given her one and would get frustrated that she wouldn't take it, again. She even talked to her like she was an adult and then became upset when Emily wouldn't answer her. I thought it was so strange when she told me Emily was mad at her and that was why she wasn't talking." Monica stopped for a moment to gather her thoughts and give Jack a chance to comment if he chose. When he remained silent she went on, "But she loved her Jack. She dressed her and kept her clean, for the most part, and we took her to a Doctor right away when we got back. I helped her to get a part time job at the bakery and she was planning on saving her money to get her own place. She even talked about you. She didn't want you to see her like she was, but made me promise to tell you about everything later, in the future, when she had her life together. It all seemed plausible and I really thought she had her head on straight, for someone who had been through what she had."

"You've got to believe me Jack, I wanted to tell you. Emily was so sweet and perfect, and I knew you had suffered so much after Mystiques disappearance." Monica said in an exasperated voice.

"She stayed with me for about a week and a half before I changed my mind about contacting someone." She went on as she stared at the blank expression on his face. "One day I came home from work and found Emily lying in her crib crying and crying, but I couldn't find Mystique anywhere. I tended to Em and waited for Mystique to come back. I thought maybe she just ran downstairs to get something, but when a couple hours had passed I panicked. I knew where her parents lived from what little she had told me so I packed up Emily and we went to their house. Mystique wasn't there, but they made me give them Emily. I hated it Jack. I never thought I was going to see her again, and I knew you would hate me forever."

She couldn't read him, other than narrowing his eyes at her after that last statement he had been pretty calm throughout the story so far. But, the next part is what scared the living daylights out of her. Clearing her throat repeatedly she slowly began again.

"The day before you texted me with the pic of Emily I had received a letter from her mom and dad." She began. This time she could see the fear in his eyes as he keyed in to the tone of her voice. Pulling the crumpled letter from her shoulder bag she handed to Jack. She had kept that letter with her every day since she had received it. She knew she had to tell Jack eventually but did not dare to leave the letter somewhere in the house where he or Emily could come across it.

With shaking hands he took the envelope from her and cautiously opened it.

Dear Jack and Monica,

As you may be well aware by now, our sweet little girl has some very odd behaviors. That doesn't mean we think any less of her or feel burdened by her in any way. She is the light of our lives and we will always cherish her. By now you know that she has left our precious granddaughter in your capable hands to raise from here on out. We want you to know that she loves that little girl and if she were able she would make the best mother in the world. It breaks our hearts to have to do this. You see, Mystique is not a well woman. She has been in and out of mental facilities most of her teenage years. She was diagnosed with Schizophrenia when she was a young teen. When she is on her meds she adjusts well and flourishes. We were very worried to let her go out into the community and start college, as you know. But, she did well. She was making good grades, had good friends, and even a wonderful boyfriend. We were so happy that she adjusted so well. Our daughter so wanted a chance at normalcy that we couldn't deny her. We thought that we were being responsible; she's been on birth control shots ever since she was diagnosed with this terrible affliction.

However, when she told us she was pregnant we knew all that was going to change. She couldn't stay on her psych meds being pregnant and we knew her hallucinations would return. That is why we took her out of school like we did. Mystique spent most of her pregnancy in an institution where she could be safe and the baby could be monitored. We found the journal she kept throughout her pregnancy. The story you may have been told is not true. She was not abducted to Colorado. After Emily was born Mystique was breast feeding so she was not able to take the same meds she had been on in the past to control her mental issues. She was better with the meds she was able to take, and had come home. Then, one day she up and left with Emily. We were devastated. She had apparently reverted back to the scheme she had come up with during her pregnancy. We had found her journal open on the bed. That is when you came in Monica, she took a bus to Colorado and called you. We want to thank you from the bottom of our hearts for your generosity and quick actions that brought her and Emily home. You know most of the story from there. When you brought Emily back to us we were so relieved. Mystique still did not show up for days after that. We never found out where she had been, and probably never will. After that we made her go back on the meds that were working for her and she stopped breast feeding. Unfortunately when her mind was clear with the right medications she would forget about having had a baby. or rather, we think she knew she was not going to be able to be the kind of mother Emily needed and found it easier if she just "forgot." We had a great time with Emily for those few weeks she was with us. Mystique was great when she acknowledged her, but for the most part she was aloof. Soon after she was back on her meds, and we thought things were going to be ok, she ran off. That's where you come in, Jack. One night she came home with enthusiasm in her voice and told us she was getting back together with you. We knew then that we had to put a stop to it. It wasn't fair to you, and it wasn't fair to Emily or Mystique. This was a period of time that she had "forgotten" about Emily, so we had to tell her all about the little baby that she seemed so surprised to see when she returned home. Again, we know she is a smart girl, and we think under it all she really did know. We then packed up our precious little granddaughter and her mother and took them to your fraternity house.

We are sorry this is how it has to be, and with time we think Mystique will "forget" all together. I know you will give Emily a good life. Please let her know that her grandparents love her, and that her mother loved her as best she could. The doctors say that Emily does not have any of the genes usually associated with schizophrenia, but you should keep in mind that there is likelihood that she could develop it in the future. Please forgive us.

Ultimately we know this is our fault, and for that we will never forgive ourselves.

Best wishes
Jasmine and Patrick.

Jack folded the lengthy letter back and placed it in the envelope before handing it to Monica without a word. They both sat there in silence for a few minutes while he let it all sink in.

"I'm sorry I couldn't just let her forget. That is why I have been taking her around Mystiques shop. I am a woman, and you know I lost a baby a long time ago Jack. That is not something you just recover from. She deserved to see Emily. But I am sorry for keeping it from you."

"Lets go home." Jack sighed as he turned the key to the ignition.

17

$\mathcal{J}$ ack rushed into the house in such a hurry Angela barely heard the 'thank you' or felt the kiss on her cheek. She sat up and rubbed her tired eyes as she watched him race down the hallway and disappear into Emily's bedroom.

"What was that all about?" She asked as Monica entered a few moments later.

"He just found out some things and needs to work through them." She said.

"Will he be alright?" She asked.

"He will be." She answered as she went down the hall to look in on her little brother.

Angela was stunned. She wasn't sure if she needed to stay or not. She definitely felt out of place at that moment. She decided that it would be best to give this family the space she felt they needed. She quietly walked down the hall to peek in and tell them goodbye but stopped when she heard the sobs. Monica and Jack were both lying on either side of Emily crying and whispering softly to each other.

Angela left before they noticed her standing there.

Angela was surprised to see Jack waiting for her in the parking lot when she got off work one evening. It had been nearly a week since she had heard from him. He hadn't been taking her calls and wouldn't return her texts. She had been beside herself with worry that he had changed his mind about her. She wasn't sure what to think as she walked slowly to her car. Jack was leaning against her hood with his hands tucked deep in his pockets. He didn't say anything when she approached but slid to one side as if inviting her to stand beside him. On the drive over he had every intention to cool things with Angela for the time being. He, Monica, and Emily had spent the past week talking with doctors and having numerous tests ran to make sure she was out of the woods. Unfortunately since her birth a new test had been developed to determine whether a person had a different gene, scientists were finding to be associated with schizophrenia. Emily had that gene. He was told by the specialist that it was not conclusive in determining whether she would develop it in the future, and he was given a lot of information to deter the development. Most of it was keeping environmental and stress factors from placing her in a situation where it might be triggered. He knew he couldn't keep her in a bubble her whole life, so he was devastated.

He and Monica hadn't spoken much since then. While he understood the reasons behind her trying to keep him and Emily from harm, he couldn't forgive her for keeping that pertinent information from him.

Jack had to break down and tell his daughter about Mystique. She had been scared at first and didn't understand about her mommy's mind being sick, but she wanted to meet her.

Reluctantly he had taken her to Mystiques parents' house.

She was having a good day, that day, and cried when she got to tell Emily she was her mother. They let her explain in her own words how she was sick and why she had to turn the care of Emily over to Jack. It was a tearful reunion, but all in all Jack felt pretty good about it. They promised to stay in touch and Emily decided that she wanted to visit with Mystique from time to time. She adored the teddy bear she gave her and was proud that she finally got to meet her mother.

"A penny for your thoughts." Angela said.

Jack pulled himself back to the present. After everything he now knew, he had decided that it wasn't fair to ask Angela to deal with whatever the future might hold for him and his daughter.

Looking into her eyes he couldn't force the words from his mouth. He turned, taking his hands from his pockets and pulled her into a firm embrace.

"You feel so good!" He said. "I'm sorry I've been out of the picture for a while. We need to talk."

Angela tensed up as he spoke those words. She had a bad feeling ever since she left him and Monica crying that night. With tears in her eyes she pulled away and nodded her head.

"Oh honey, don't do that." He said as the tears sprung to his eyes as well.

With frustration he wiped them away. He had cried more since he met this woman than he remembered doing in his entire life. *I hope I can endure all this damn emotion for the rest of my life.* He thought to himself. Then he smiled and took her hand.

"Let's go for ice cream." he said.

That made Angela feel a little better. Ice cream was a happy food right? No one broke up over ice cream, they just ate it by the bucketful's after the deed was done.

They left her car in the parking lot and went back in the shopping center. After they got their orders they sat in a quiet booth in the back and she listened as he told his story.

Midway through his tale, and his ice cream, Angela wiped away a chocolate drip that had made its way out the side of his mouth. He stopped, kissed her fingers, and started again.

"So there it is." He said when he finally finished. "I wanted to be honest and tell you everything. If you don't want to marry me after this I will understand."

Angela stared at him in bewilderment for a moment. Then she slid out of her side of the booth and slid in beside him. Hugging him tightly to her, she kissed his face.

"Jack, I am so sorry all this is happening and has happened. It scares me to death to think of poor Emily having to deal with that. But you have to believe me. I am in this for the long haul. I love you. I want to be with you totally and completely. I love Emily and I want to be there for her too." She said between kisses.

"That is the best news I've heard in a long time!" He said as he hugged her even tighter.

Angela went to Jacks house for supper that night. She and Emily had fun making lasagna and garlic bread, all from scratch.

"Mmmmmm, this sure is good girls. I think I'll hire you both on to do the cooking from now on!" Jack said with a wink to Angela.

"Oh daddy, you know I can cook. I learned it from Aunt Monica." Emily said.

Jack knew it hurt her that Monica hadn't been around lately. He knew he had to find a way to forgive his sister. He was all set to make amends when the test results came back telling him that Emily could possibly share the same fate as her mother. In his mind he knew that finding this out sooner wouldn't have made any difference in how he had raised her so far, but he was a stubborn man and couldn't let go of the grudge he held just yet. Instead of commenting about Monica he opted to change the subject.

"Why don't you ladies set up a board game in the living room while I clean up these dirty dishes." He said as he stood and rubbed his belly all the while sticking it out as far as he could.

"If you keep feeding me like that I might get mistaken for Jolly old Saint Nick!" He joked as he started gathering plates and glasses to put in the sink.

At the end of the evening Jack walked Angela to her car. There was a warm breeze blowing as they strolled hand in hand down the stone walkway.

"This was nice." She said. "I really enjoyed myself. Thank you for letting me spend the evening with you and Emily."

"Thank you for everything." He said in reply. "You have really helped me relax and forget about things."

Angela looked around the neighborhood at all the pretty houses lit up with Christmas lights. Smiling she looked back at him with tears in her eyes.

"What is it?" He asked leaning closer and pulling her into his arms.

"This is just so wonderful, It just feels so right, you, Emily, us. I can't imagine my life without it." She said.

"I know just what you mean." He whispered in her hair as he held her tighter.

18

"It was so nice of your boss to let us use his house for our anniversary party." Gretchen said as she walked by the mirror checking her reflection for the third time in less than five minutes.

"Mom, stop pacing! You look beautiful. Dad is going to be so happy to have such a gorgeous bride by his side tonight." Angela said as she admired the diamond earrings her mother had found on her nightstand when she woke this morning.

"Dad has good taste mom. Who would have thought?" She said

Gretchen put her palms to her ears and smiled.

"Now get out of that gown. You are not wearing that to the play at church. All the other women would have to go home in shame!" Angela said as she pushed her mother toward the bathroom.

"Did you know your boss lived in such a place?" Gretchen hollered from her vanity in the bathroom.

"I didn't have a clue mom, but apparently he comes from money. That house is a mansion and I just saw the first two floors." She yelled back before deciding to get closer so they wouldn't have to shout.

"Well, honey you saved his life. Let's live it up like royalty and reap the benefits of his generosity." She yelled back.

"Mom, I'm right here." Angela said.

Gretchen jumped. "I'm sorry sweetheart; I thought you were still in the bedroom."

"Mom, I have some big news. Two things actually." She said with a big grin on her face.

"Well, don't keep me in suspense honey, go on." Gretchen urged.

"Jack and I have been talking about marriage." She said and squealed causing her mother to start jumping up and down and squeal too.

"That is fantastic news honey. I knew it the minute I saw him on the plane that night. That man wasn't letting you go." Her mother said when she finally stopped jumping around.

"When's the wedding? Did you get a ring? How did he propose? Are you going to stay in Lacasine?" She rambled.

"Whoa mom. One question at a time." Angela said with a laugh.

"We're just talking and nothing is official yet, no ring, and of course we will stay here, our families are here and Emily is already in school here." She said.

"Ohhhhh, I forgot about that little one!" Gretchen squealed again as she started jumping up and down for the second time. "She'll be my grandbaby!"

Stopping her flouncing around and becoming deadly silent Gretchen stared at Angela for a minute. It was almost eerie, she had never seen that look on her mother's face before.

"What is it mom?" She asked.

"That's the second part isn't it? Are you pregnant young lady?" Her mother questioned.

"No, no, I am not mom, that is not why we are getting married and that is not the second part." She consoled while patting her mother's shaking hands she had been wringing together.

"My boss asked me to be Assistant Manager of The Dress Barn." She stated bluntly.

"Oh honey, that's terrific!" Gretchen said as she started getting dressed again.

"I decided not to take it mom; I'm going back to school. I'll stay there, just not as their assistant manager." She gushed.

"Oh?" Gretchen became nervous again.

Angela could see the fear building in her Mothers face for the second time in less than a minute so she continued. "I'm still staying here mom, I have been thinking about going into the medical field. I know it is completely different than what I originally went to school for, but I really feel that is my calling, I love helping those little old ladies at the Dress barn, and I love helping with the little girls at church. I think I want to help people rather than just dress them up. I have signed up for the Nurse Assistant classes at the community college. Heck, maybe I'll even be a nurse or a doctor, who knows."

Gretchen kissed her daughter on the forehead. She was proud of her.

— ~

The church play went on without a hitch Emily and Becca did a wonderful job with their parts and Angela made a beautiful angel. The church was packed.

When it was finished Emily ran to Monica, who was sitting beside Wendi, Becca's mother, across the church from Jack.

"We did it! And did you see my pretty angel?" She asked Monica.

"I did honey, I saw all of you." She replied.

"You made a wonderful Inn Keeper, and Becca here was a good Shepard." Wendi said.

"Well, that's cause the boys didn't want to be in a dumb old play they said. But we did, and we did good!" Emily went on as she took her friends arm and led them all to where Jack and Angela were.

"Thanks for letting me watch Emily tonight." Monica said in a somber voice as she approached her brother.

"It's fine, bring her back in the morning." He mumbled without looking at her. He then leaned down and kissed Emily on the cheek and told her she did a great job.

He was out of the sanctuary before Monica could get another word in.

Angela smiled to try and console her and mouthed the word 'sorry' as she followed Jack outside. Her parents were waiting with him.

"Let's get this show on the road!" Ken said. "Our chariot awaits."

They had all four piled into his Camaro and he couldn't wait to get back behind the wheel.

— —

"I think that's the fastest you have ever changed clothes in all our married life!" Ken whispered to Gretchen as they entered the beautiful mansion.

"Welcome folks!" Mr. Montgomery said as the butler showed them in.

Angela was amazed that her boss lived like this. The mansion was on the outskirts of Crowley sat upon ten acres. There had been a gated entry and a long winding path brilliantly lit with Christmas lights. But, when they got inside she saw the real magnificence of it. The butlers were dressed in top hats and coats with tails. One had led them to a well-lit dining area. Crystal chandeliers shimmered as candlelight danced on the silk table cloths and red roses that filled every table. Ken and Gretchen's friends were already seated and all stood to applaud when then entered.

"Mr. Montgomery, this is too much!" Angela whispered as she stood back to watch her parents bask in the spotlight.

"Nothing of it! It was my pleasure." He said and walked briskly to his wife who was greeting Angela's parents.

"Oh Jack, do you think we will be that happy in thirty-five years?" She asked in wonderment as she watched her parents.

"We will." He said as he pulled a little black velvet box from his coat pocket. "Will you marry me my Angel?"

"Oh Jack! Yes, yes I will!" She answered.

Epilogue

Jack and Angela officially announced their engagement at Christmas, although most everyone seemed to already be aware. Angela had a feeling her mother hadn't kept their little chat a secret for very long. After their short courtship, they decided a long engagement wouldn't hurt. Angela moved in with Jack and Emily the following spring and they waited to get married for what they thought was the perfect day.

Angela had taken a job as a nurse's assistant in a local nursing home after completing her C.N.A. training. She loved the work and had plans to go on to nursing school when the spring semester started in January. She was never bothered again by her ex-boyfriend who was spending his time in federal prison for all the crimes that had eventually caught up with him.

Jacks parents, as well as Angela's, were happy for their children, and all four of them were hinting for more grandchildren right away.

Denver and Ricky had been through some rigorous marriage counseling and things seemed to be looking up. They were expecting a new addition to their family in March.

Emily was flourishing in school. She had exceptional grades, and had taken a liking to art, which was something she could share with Mystique. The two of them enjoyed classes in sculpture and painting at the local YMCA when Mystique was having a 'good' day. Emily proudly wore the ring that brought everything full circle, on a chain around her neck. It made the two of them feel comforted that she always had something with her that had once belonged to her biological mother. Angela and Jack made sure she was at all her Dr appointments. There hadn't been anything yet to show she would develop the illness her biological mother had, but they made sure they were staying on top of things.

Amos and Monica had started dating that summer and were engaged to be married around Christmas time.

Jack still wasn't able to fully forgive Monica, but they had a decent relationship, and for that they were both grateful.

Halloween was the day it all started so it only seemed fitting for them to exchange their vows on that day. They were married in a beautiful ceremony held on the grounds of her former boss's estate.

"Thank you for giving me my Angel daddy, I love her." Emily said as she danced with Jack at the extravagant wedding ceremony that made her and Angela feel like royalty. Mr. Montgomery and his wife had gone all out to give his former employee the wedding of her dreams. It was only but a small token of a gift compared to the gift she had given them by saving his life.

"Me too princess, me too." Jack said.

About the Author

Chelle Renee is, first and foremost, a lover and maker of words. She doesn't remember a time when she didn't write, and this passion has led to several of her poems being published in magazines and websites. In 2007, she won the Missouri Health Care Association Essay contest. It was a fitting award, given her eighteen years of experience in health care.

When she isn't writing, she works as a nurse in a residential care facility, and she and her husband live in the beautiful Ozarks.

44093000R00083

Made in the USA
Lexington, KY
07 July 2019